Unexpectedly Expecting

The Sheik's Baby

The Ladies of the Burling School

Elizabeth Lennox

Table of Contents

Chapter 1

"Please don't look in my office," Cassandra Flemming whispered as she balanced the heavy case files she'd brought home last night. Unfortunately, the rush was needed since she was late for work. Again!

"*Please* be too busy to look in my office!" Cassy prayed under her breath as she hurried down the long hallway, ignoring the pinch in her shoes and the tight band around her waist since she'd accidentally pulled on the suit that she'd banished to the back of her closet after she'd gained too much weight to comfortably wear it. Unfortunately, she hadn't brought her other suits to the drycleaners over the past two weeks, so this suit was all that was clean.

Juggling several files, her computer, a gym bag, and the extra-large tote bag that served as her purse, she hurried through the maze of hallways to her tiny office, keeping her eyes forward so she didn't have to acknowledge her coworkers already at their desks, heads down and working diligently. She wasn't *extremely* late. But even five minutes after the stroke of eight o'clock in the morning would cause her boss to issue a demoralizing reprimand. Usually, those admonishments happened in front of her co-workers, which made the scolding ten times worse.

It didn't matter that Cassy was late because she'd only gotten two hours of sleep last night. It didn't matter that she'd e-mailed a very important brief to her boss at four o'clock this morning, a brief that had been dumped on her desk yesterday after five o'clock. After finishing that assignment, Cassy had leaned back in her uncomfortable kitchen chair to rest her eyes "just for a moment" before heading to bed – which caused her to fall asleep in said chair. And since she'd fallen asleep in the kitchen, she hadn't heard her alarm go off in her bedroom at six o'clock this morning.

Hence, why she was late.

Unfortunately, the fact that she'd worked twenty-one hours the day before had little bearing on the fact that she was fifteen minutes late today.

"Ms. Flemming," a condescending and clearly irritated male voice barked barely a fraction of a second after she'd entered her office. Thankfully, Cassy had already put both of her cumbersome bags down and turned around, still holding the file folders confidently in her arms.

"Mr. Hanover!" she replied with her shoulders back and head held high, as if she were eager to see the man. She took the top file folder off of her stack. "The Osaka briefing is right here, although I also e-mailed it to you last night." He opened his mouth to say something, but Cassy didn't give him a chance. "The argument I compiled is powerful and I've found several cases to back up the defense." He glanced down at the file, his mouth still open, but Cassy wasn't going to endure any sort of tardiness reprimand! Not after the work she'd done last night. It was good stuff. She might be exhausted, but she was a damn good lawyer!

Instead of waiting for him to speak, she handed him the next file, explaining rapidly, unaware of the sparkle of excitement in her eyes. "I won the Simms case yesterday, but I wrote a follow up summary with all the issues we confronted during the trial, as well as a list of problems we might want to e-mail our clients in similar situations. The problems this defendant faced during court will come up again in several of the cases we are working right now. I've summarized the problems and how I solved them, then e-mailed them to each of the lawyers, as well as copying you so you're fully up to date."

She handed him the last file, which was the biggest, and continued, "This was the most interesting case and I cited several problems with the treaty. And let me say thank you *so* much for letting me review it. International law is the area I'd like to specialize in."

Ian Hanover was obviously flustered as he accepted the case files, trying to balance each of them as Cassy handed them over while still listening to her explanations. "Ms. Flemming!" he finally interrupted. It only worked because Cassy was finished.

"Yes?" she asked, proud of the work she'd done during the previous twenty-four hours. Those briefs weren't written by a bimbo. She'd worked long hours and done a huge amount of tedious, exhaustive research. Everything was summarized with exemplary writing and she hadn't relaxed until each bullet point was succinct and powerful. No superfluous wording in her briefs. Everything was straight to the point. Just like her.

Cassy might struggle with timeliness, especially when she had to work until the wee hours of the morning, but she was a darn good lawyer!

With a sigh, Mr. Hanover waved the files in his hands to interrupt her. "You are needed in conference room six," he said, tucking the files under his arm and frowning at her, his voice lowering in an attempt to convey the importance of this news. "This is a very important client. As such, you will stay with the members of this meeting for the whole day, advising them on any international issues that come up. Darren Meyers will also be in the room. He has more experience, but these are," he paused to close her office door and dropped his voice to continue, "extremely sensitive meetings. I must remind you of the non-disclosure agreement you signed when you joined this firm, as well as your absolute adherence to the lawyer-client privilege. Nothing, and I mean *nothing*, can be discussed outside of that conference room. Any conversations you have with the participants of that room must remain confidential as well. All information concerning these meetings will be kept in a secure location, known only to the participants of that room and this law office. Do I make myself clear?"

Cassy straightened her spine even more, feeling excitement bubble up inside her. This was her break! This was her chance to show the world she was a good lawyer and not just...!

"Yes sir," she replied. She self-consciously tugged her black suit jacket down.

Mr. Hanover peered at her through his thick glasses for a moment before accepting her assurance. "Good. Then get in there. The participants should be arriving shortly. The conference room is ready for you."

Cassy grabbed a new pad of legal paper as well as several pens, and hurried down the hallway. She slipped through the door and nodded to the other lawyers that were milling about. Darren, one of the other lawyers working his way through the sometimes confusing maze towards a coveted partnership with the firm, was already there. As usual, his smug, entitled expression was present as he watched her walk through the conference room doors, his red suspenders and blue striped shirt showing off his pretentious and self-important nature.

"Hello there, beautiful," he greeted Cassy, using that smarmy smile that he clearly thought was charming. "How about drinks after this shindig? It sounds like we're going to need something to stimulate our minds."

Cassy walked over to one of the chairs and set her notepad and pens down before turning to Darren, feeling proud of herself for not rolling her eyes. "Thank you, but I have plans."

Darren followed her, standing too close and trying to tower over her.

3

Unfortunately for him, Darren stood only a few inches taller than her five foot, six inch height. When she wore heels, Cassy topped him by an inch and she knew that he hated that. So Cassy turned and stared down her nose at him, ensuring that the jerk knew that she wasn't going to play his games today. Well, she never played his games. Right now, he was trying to invade her space, intimidate her. But Cassy had stopped being unsettled by bullies like this a long time ago! He was the kind of guy that needed to intimidate women to feel powerful and it was annoying.

"Ditch him," Darren argued immediately. "I'm a much more *generous* lover." He skimmed his fingers down her arm.

Cassy cringed, pulling back with disgust that she could barely keep from her expression. "No thanks. And don't ever touch me like that again." She added a firm glare to back up her words.

Before Darren could rally, there was a commotion at one of the doorways and Cassy breathed a sigh of relief. Now that they were no longer alone, Darren wouldn't make any other skeevy comments or gestures. He was sleazy and impossibly forward, but this was a conservative, powerful firm with a large number of powerful, male lawyers.

Confidently, she turned to face the newcomers and she pasted on a professional smile.

She was glad she was standing by one of the tall leather chairs surrounding the conference room table because the man who walked in was possibly the most astonishing male she'd ever seen. He was impossibly tall. But more than that, he was...wow, there really were no words. "Harsh" popped into her mind. Yes, harsh and erotic.

Was that even possible? Her brain fizzled as she gripped the back of the chair, trying to stop herself from tipping over. She'd seen handsome men before. Darren was considered attractive physically. It was his personality that Cassy found repulsive. But this stranger, this giant specimen of masculinity was not normal. There was something so...raw about him. Raw and...harsh, she thought again.

His face was angular with a hawk-like nose and black hair. His eyes appeared to be black, but that might have just been the lighting. He was also impressively tan and had unbelievably broad shoulders. Everything about him screamed "power". Harsh power, she thought. Ferocious power!

He shook hands with the senior partners and began discussing something quietly so Cassy had several minutes to get herself under control. Breathe, she reminded herself silently. Just breathe.

In that same moment, he turned and looked right at her. Those eyes! His dark gaze grabbed her, held her hostage in an almost sensuous way.

She couldn't move, couldn't look away. Everything faded to a hazy blur except for this man.

He came closer. With every step, she felt her heart pounding harder, crashing against her ribs. Surely, the whole room could hear her heart pounding!

He walked like a panther stalking his pray, moving closer while holding her gaze. By the time he reached her, she was trembling. And instead of a steady, pounding heart, she felt it racing.

Gone was the sophisticated, hard-driving lawyer, Cassandra had worked so hard over the years to portray, and live up to that image. But with only a few steps into the room, this man, this ferocious beast, had demolished that image, replacing it with...something else. Something softer. She didn't like it!

"This is Ms. Cassandra Flemming. She and Mr. Meyers will be sitting in to advise on issues and to answer any questions," the lead partner explained.

Mr. Ferocious shook Darren's hand first and Cassy breathed a sigh of relief. He and Darren exchanged a few words, but Cassy knew what would happen next and braced herself as he turned those dark eyes on her. Darren bowed slightly.

"Ms. Flemming," he said, her name a soft caress as he reached for her hand.

Cassy extended her hand, praying that he wouldn't notice the trembling. Unfortunately, the moment their skin touched, she felt an electric shock run up her arm. She tried to hide her reaction, but those eyes caught her surprised expression, as well as the slight jerk at his touch. His hand holding hers captive wasn't warm, it was hot! And it held hers firmly, his other hand coming to cover her fingers. Cassy felt trapped, but in a way that she didn't want to escape. While the rational part of her mind told her to step back, another part, the part of her that was inexplicably fascinated by him, wanted to step closer.

Thankfully, a noise from the other entrance startled her enough to break the spell and she pulled her hand away. Turning around, she gripped the back of the chair, not sure why she felt so dizzy. She worked with men all day long, worked out at the gym with men and swarmed the sidewalks and subway system with men all the time. Why was this man, who was now standing so close behind her that she could feel the heat from his body against her back even through the thick layers of her wool suit, further crumbling her defenses? What kind of magic did he have?

The senior partner stepped up and made the introductions to the newcomers. Darren, always the opportunist, introduced himself, sticking his hand out quickly to be the first. "It is an honor, Your Highness," he said, bowing again.

'Your Highness'? Cassy tried to step away, needing to process, but the heat of Mr. Ferocious ensnared her. She realized that she'd just backed up into him and tried to step away, only he put a hand to her shoulder, pulling her back. The trembling that had begun the moment he'd stepped into the conference room increased, leaving her fighting to breathe. She looked down at the carpet, trying to regain control but, even though his hand was no longer there, she could still feel his touch, and knew that he was right there, holding her prisoner.

"Nasir," a tall, handsome man came forward. "I see you have already made a productive acquisition," the new man said with amusement sparkling in his eyes.

Cassy looked up and found that the man was looking directly at her, his startlingly golden eyes dancing. Oddly, although this man was just as tall and intimidating as the man behind her, Cassy didn't feel the same shocking current as she extended her hand when introduced to him.

"You understand the situation correctly, Mikal," Nasir del Soya Irazi replied, his dark eyes daring the other man. The two men spoke in Arabic though, to maintain their privacy. He suspected that capturing the interest of the woman trembling in front of him would be much more of a challenge than his previous conquests, and the thought pleased him inordinately.

Sheik Mikal el Diarasi chuckled and eyed the woman again. "Your choice is clear, my friend. I would not dare to get in your way. And I applaud your choice. She will give you strong children to carry on your legacy."

Nasir glanced at the lovely Cassandra Flemming again, noting the flare of emotion in her dark eyes, the glossy shine of her hair. He wanted to release her hairpins and see her hair dance around her shoulders. A baby machine? Nasir could see the intelligence in her eyes and knew that she was so much more. Plus, he doubted the lovely lady would enjoy being reduced to a baby factory, so he didn't translate Mikal's comment.

Still, he wanted to take her hand again and reassure her. He could see the trembling in her shoulders as she struggled to maintain a professional demeanor. Her presence here in this room indicated that she had a strong legal mind. These meetings today were to forge an agreement between two countries. Both he and Mikal had demanded the expertise of this firm because of the firm's reputation. The lawyers employed here would be the best, so Ms. Flemming wasn't just a lovely woman. She was likely a powerful force in the legal world.

A part of him wanted to walk away from Ms. Flemming, to ignore the potent pull he felt. He had enough challenges in his life, he didn't need more. But there was no denying the attraction he felt. In fact, he'd never felt this kind of attraction before. There was no chance of ignoring the increasing awareness.

Cassy wondered what they were saying. It was the height of rudeness to speak in a foreign language, especially since she was certain they were talking about her!

"Excuse me," she interrupted. "I need to..."

"You need to stay right where you are, my little one," the man behind her said.

His voice sounded like sandpaper with a large dose of menace mixed in, but somehow it smoothed over her skin like satin, sending additional shivers right down to her stomach. The shivers weren't such a horrible issue. It was the throbbing lower, deeper than her stomach, which worried her and forced her shoulders to stiffen. She was not that kind of woman, she reminded herself.

And "my little one"? Who the hell did he think he was?! She wasn't his property! And "little"? She wasn't little! She was average height! Definitely not little!

She felt him move behind her slightly. Okay, maybe she was little compared to him. He was ridiculously tall, well over six feet. Still...! She wasn't his little anything!

With stiff, insulted outrage, Cassy stalked towards the end of the table. She knew that the firm's partners would be sitting at the other end while she and Darren took notes and offered suggestions during the breaks. She was also here to observe and pass those observations to the others. She'd done this before during other negotiations, so she knew the drill. Still, she couldn't wait for the day when she was the one sitting at the other end of the table.

Cassy wanted to glare at the tall, ferocious man, but knew that he was an important client, so she settled for cold professionalism as she sat down in one of the expensive leather chairs.

And she'd prove to the big jerk that she was a damn good lawyer and not his personal plaything!

Nasir watched the woman walk away. He could sense her anger. His gaze took in her figure, irritated that he could see so little of it. The collar of her black, wool suit came up to her chin and the skirt ended a few inches below her knees. Her shoes were conservative and boring, but nothing could hide her elegant silhouette. As she walked, the suit moved with her, revealing the round curve of her bottom. Her breasts were a strange shape, he noticed, wondering why. He could tell that she was slender by the delicate bone structure in her face. Her high cheekbones enhanced her expressive dark eyes, which flashed with fire when she was angry, and also revealed exactly what she was feeling. The two of them had an interesting connection, a chemistry that would not only work into his plans perfectly, but would add an enjoyable spark into his future.

"Ah, here is Tarek," Mikal said, speaking in English now. "I don't believe he has made the same progress as you."

Nasir watched as the introductions were made to the third, and final, member of their group. He nodded with satisfaction when the beautiful woman took Tarek's hand. There was no spark there either, although Tarek immediately noticed the woman's exceptional beauty beneath the hideous suit. The other men in the room had as well. He supposed he'd have to get used to other men looking at her. She really was startlingly lovely, even if she tried to hide her beauty.

He'd have to find out why, he mused as the three men took seats around the table. The extraneous people left the room, leaving only himself, Tarek, Mikal, and the two lawyers. A recorder in the center of the table was there to record the meeting, which would be transcribed later.

"Let's get down to business," he announced, starting the meeting.

Cassy turned to a fresh page in her notebook and began taking notes, while wondering what was going on with these three men. It seemed serious. They discussed historical borders, oil prices, real estate costs, and a slew of other issues. Occasionally, the debate became tense, but the three, speaking in English now, managed to calm down and find a compromise every time the conversation grew heated. And when they could, it felt as if all three were willing to concede key arguments. By the time lunch was brought in, the men appeared to be in good moods.

Cassy's tension, on the other hand, had only increased throughout the morning. Between trying to interpret the legal issues and offer advice when requested, she could feel the intensity rise and fall in the room.

Occasionally, Mr. Ferocious glanced in her direction, his dark gaze reminding her that he was fully aware of her presence. Every time that happened, her heart stumbled slightly and she had to look away. And darn it, her hands refused to stop shaking! She pushed her chair back from the table and slid her notebook onto her lap, hiding her hands.

Cassy definitely did not want him to realize how much he affected her. The other three seemed oblivious to the tension between them. Mr. Ferocious, on the other hand, was not only aware of the tension, he encouraged it. She could tell.

Thankfully, he was at an angle where no one noticed when he looked at her, but every time she felt his eyes, she would look up and feel the heat of his gaze emanating towards her. She didn't understand how he could have this much of an impact on her. The other two men occasionally looked at her when they asked her a question or when she clarified a legal issue, but she didn't feel that electric shock lance through her when they looked at her.

When the lunch cart was delivered, everyone stood up to stretch their legs and to speak with their staff members who had been delegated to the outside chairs against the walls. They hadn't been allowed to speak during the negotiations, but they seemed to be frantically taking notes.

When the participants stood up, she breathed a sigh of relief, thinking to slip away and find a few moments of peace, a precious fifteen minutes to pull herself together. The man's staff seemed to almost sprint towards him, eager to speak to him.

He lifted his hand, almost casually, and the staff members faded back against the wall. None disobeyed and Cassy's stomach muscles tensed. She tried to get away, turning towards the door at the other end of the conference room. Regrettably, her attempts were foiled.

"Miss Flemming," that voice called out from behind her.

Cassy's shoulders tightened with that deep, rough voice and she turned around. Sure enough, it was him. He was so close, she took a step back and froze when he put a hand on her upper arm, holding her in place just as his touch had done earlier.

"Ms. Flemming," she corrected, standing as calmly as possible with her hands folded in front of her. Because she wanted to reach out to touch him, to feel that heat once again, she curled her fingers tightly together.

He cocked an eyebrow as he accepted two filled plates from his assistant. "You are divorced?" he asked, handing her a china plate filled with the kinds of foods one would expect in a gourmet, high end restaurant. She'd definitely never participated in a meeting where food of this quality was served. Cassy wished she had the strength to turn down the offering, thinking it would be more appropriate if she got her own. But she hadn't eaten breakfast this morning since she'd been running late so she took the plate, feeling silly since her hands were still shaking.

It wasn't because of this man's nearness, she told herself. She was simply intimidated by the power surrounding her. She hadn't understood at the beginning of the meeting, but now that she'd been listening

9

in for several hours, she grasped that these three men were sheiks, rulers of their countries, and were setting the stage for tricky trade deals between their three countries.

She appreciated the historic nature of these talks and was awed by the scope, amazed that the three leaders seemed to be truly eager to forge a deal and thrilled to be a part of such an historic moment.

Regardless, her excitement at being a part of this conversation didn't diminish her sense of danger when this man looked at her. There was just...just something about him. Something she didn't understand, something that tugged at her senses even as her instincts screamed to keep him at a distance.

As she looked up at him, she knew that she wouldn't be able to control this man like she controlled the men she'd dated in the past. She would be vulnerable to him in ways she didn't completely understand.

Cassy nervously accepted the offered plate, looking down at the food as her stomach warned her that it wouldn't be patient. "No. I go by Ms. and not Miss."

He shifted, almost as if he was trying to isolate them from the others in the conference room. Cassy looked around, but the man was so tall and his shoulders so broad, she couldn't really see around him without being obvious.

"I don't understand. I thought the appropriate greeting was 'Miss' for unmarried women, 'Mrs.' for married, and 'Ms.' for those who are divorced. Am I incorrect?"

Cassy flushed and looked down again. "In a few industries, that is still correct, but women in the corporate world have taken over the 'Ms.' and use it interchangeably. Our marital status should not be brought up in the workplace. It isn't relevant to anyone but ourselves."

Was that amusement she saw in his eyes? She bristled slightly, thinking that the man was humoring her. She didn't like that, especially when discussing such an important issue that provided a necessary, psychological equalizer.

"Ah, but a woman should be proud of her marital state," he countered, putting a hand to her elbow to lead her towards the opposite end of the table, where they could eat in relative privacy.

Cassy shook her head, and sank into the leather chair gratefully because she wasn't sure how much longer her legs would hold her up. Not with him so close and with that warm hand on her arm.

She tried to scoot her chair further away, but he followed so that their legs remained perilously close together. If she shifted in any way, she was in danger of her knee touching his thigh. She couldn't allow that!

Shifting her focus away from the proximity of their legs and back to his dark, too-knowing eyes, she realized that he was fully aware of her maneuvering. Instead of telling him off, and possibly getting herself fired for that telling-off, she focused instead on his question.

"I disagree. A woman should be proud of how she contributes to the world and her community," she argued. "Her marital status is a private matter between herself and her husband. It isn't anyone else's business."

Nasir was having a great deal of fun. He could see the anger in her eyes and enjoyed the sparkle. Her cheeks were pink with her fire as well. He actually had three women in his cabinet and they were a strong part of his group of advisors. Those women worked hard to promote gender equality in his country, although he was the first to acknowledge that there was still a long way to go. Which could also be said of her country, but admitting that wouldn't be nearly as fun.

"Isn't marriage a woman's ultimate goal?"

Cassy rolled her eyes. "Absolutely not! A woman can contribute just as much as a man." Her lips pressed together and she dropped her gaze to her hands folded in her lap. Well, not exactly folded. Her fingers were gripping each other in an effort to not gesture wildly. "But perhaps we will just have to agree to disagree on this subject."

"And where do you stand on the question of marriage? Do you reject marriage completely or are you just against anyone in your professional realm knowing about your marital status?"

Nasir watched her mouth, fascinated and intrigued. She was such a sensuous beauty and yet, she tried to hide it behind a stiff, starched suit. The contrast between her pale skin, full mouth, and sparkling eyes compared to that hideous suit was fascinating. She probably had no idea that her efforts at minimizing her femininity only enhanced it.

Cassy laughed, finally understanding that he was teasing her. With that laughter, her irritation over his sexist comments dissipated. How could he do that so easily? One moment, she was ready to kick him and the next, she could read the teasing glint in his eyes. It was oddly flattering that he would tease her.

Shaking her head, she took a deep breath. "I beg your pardon, Your Highness, but why do you care about my opinion on marriage? It really isn't relevant."

Nasir leaned back, shrugging one shoulder. "It might be more relevant than you think."

He took a bite of his lunch and changed the subject. Once they were on more neutral subjects, Nasir noticed she relaxed and he enjoyed the way she laughed occasionally, and how her eyes sparkled when she became irritated. He appreciated that she wasn't afraid to argue with him, that she challenged him. That was a good sign. It was rare that someone in her position felt comfortable enough to make a point and speak openly. She was refreshing. Even more so since his interest was obvious and yet, she didn't throw herself at him, or drop hints that she was his for the taking. Even more of a challenge, he thought with growing interest.

They conversed throughout the rest of the meal, but too soon, the lunch break was over and he needed to consult with his aides before resuming the meeting for their afternoon session.

Lifting her hand, he kissed her fingertips, then turned her hand over and placed another kiss on the delicate skin of her wrist, tightening his grip when he felt her shiver and try to pull away. Cassandra must have understood the look in his eyes. He felt the trembling and noticed that she held her breath for a long moment. She wasn't sure how to react and that gave him a slight pause. She wasn't as experienced as his previous lovers, Nasir realized. Ms. Cassandra Flemming was a beautiful mixture of innocence and experience.

Cassy was starting to hate the effect that deep, masculine voice had on her. And he kissed her wrist! Who did that? She'd seen it in the movies, but...in real life?

"I enjoyed our meal together, Ms. Flemming. Thank you for a delightful respite from the tense negotiations today." With that, he stepped back, bowed ever so slightly and then moved off to discuss something with his aides who were waiting patiently by one of the large windows of the conference room.

Cassy watched, fascinated by the body language and the man. The others seemed to be offering him advice and the tall, dangerous man listened intently, but with a look about him that clearly conveyed that he wasn't making any decisions just yet.

"Looks like you made a conquest," Darren commented as he sauntered over to stand beside her. "Guess I wasn't wealthy enough." He snorted at his comment and Cassy looked over at the smoothly professional man just as he shook his head, glaring at their client.

"A conquest?" she asked, her shoulders stiffening at the insinuation.

Darren looked at her with an expression of...triumph? Maybe revulsion? Immediately, something shriveled up inside of her. Was he implying that she...that he...? Her eyes moved from Darren's blue ones to the darker gaze watching them. She had no idea that her mouth had fallen open slightly in response to her co-worker's awful comments.

Nor did she realize that the taller man seemed to understand what was being said simply by the way her shoulders curled in slightly, as if protecting herself.

Darren understood Nasir's furious glare and jerked to attention as Nasir whispered something to his aide. Cassy was completely unaware of the silent messages being sent and absorbed across the polished conference room table. But she definitely understood that Darren was implying that she had...that Nasir was sexually interested in her.

Okay, so that was pretty obvious, if not from the soft touches earlier, the kiss on her wrist was an obvious clue.

But Cassy knew she hadn't done anything inappropriate. She'd done her best to avoid him without insulting him. He was an important client! Thinking over the morning's interactions, she knew she hadn't done anything wrong. Other than the soft kiss on her wrist, which still tingled, there had been nothing inappropriate about her interactions.

Of course, her thoughts had been another matter entirely! Cassy was fairly confident that none of the other people in the room were aware of those thoughts.

Which made Darren's insinuations completely unfounded and rude! Was she going to have to say something? She glanced over at Nasir again, the man who was more powerful than she could even imagine. Had he perhaps said something to someone else that might have hurt her career? Had Darren...

A slight shake of his head told her to stop thinking along those lines. Cassy looked away, horrified that he could so easily read her mind.

Unfortunately, Darren's comments gnawed at her. A conquest? What had she done wrong? And how could she fix it? She thought back over the morning, trying to figure out what she'd done and how she could have handled the situation differently. She couldn't simply ignore the problem. Assumptions of this magnitude could destroy one's career and she'd worked too hard for too long to let it go.

Unfortunately, the meeting was called back to order and she walked across the room, trying to keep her head held high, but she felt...dirty somehow. She'd done absolutely nothing wrong and yet, the men around her had sullied her reputation. Over an innocent conversation!

Granted, the subtle, non-verbal messages hadn't been exactly innocent but...the others in the room couldn't know that. Could they?

The meeting restarted and Cassy sat down, shaking again but this time for a completely different reason. For the rest of the afternoon, she refused to look at Nasir.

Had she done or said something to indicate that she was interested? Had Darren caught one of her glances?

If that were the case, then she would have to be extra careful during the afternoon session. She simply wouldn't look at Nasir. When he asked her a question, she looked at her notes, pretending to verify the information written there.

Issue after issue was discussed in a seemingly never-ending meeting. Cassy wondered if anyone else needed a break. Unfortunately, as she glanced around the room, everyone seemed fresh and engaged.

Looking down at her paper, she tried to focus only on the words and not on Darren's sneering presence beside her. When the meeting was finally over, she waited just long enough for the clients to leave before she hurried out of the conference room. She didn't want to wait around for Darren's next comment or for someone to ask her what was going on between herself and an obviously important client. Cassy refused to even listen to such horrible insinuations, especially from Darren, who thought that women were his personal playthings. He had no respect for women and he was a married man! So how dare he imply that she'd behaved inappropriately towards a client!

With her head down, she rushed into her office, determined to get away and rebalance herself. Grabbing her gym bag and her black tote, she hurried out of the building, without stopping to talk to anyone. She didn't check her e-mail, nor did she care if there was a stack of issues that needed her attention. She wanted out! She needed some breathing space!

When she was on the street, her cell phone rang. "Hey, where are you?" Ella asked. "Naya and I are in the lobby waiting for you."

Cassy continued down the street, not looking around as she maintained her furious pace. "I'm on my way to the gym. I'll meet you guys there."

She was already warming up when her friends slipped into the large aerobics class area. "Okay, what's going on?" Ella asked, dumping her bag by the doorway. "You never beat us to class. Usually, we have to text you to get your butt down here."

Ella was the most direct of their trio. As a news reporter, she traveled all over the world, ferreting out the next scoop and revealing the bad guys and their illegal antics. It was pretty rare when Ella could meet them for class, but whenever Ella was home, the three of them made the most out of their time together.

Naya walked in next, breathless and tugging her shirt down over her hips. Naya was the most voluptuous of their group, and also the shyest. She fought her natural instincts to retreat into her own world, wanting to be more extroverted. Naya was brilliantly creative, and preferred her world of colors and subtle marketing tactics.

14

Cassy looked at her two friends, not really sure what to say. In the end, she simply grabbed at the first excuse she knew they would accept. "I was in a meeting all day with Darren. First thing he said this morning, before the clients arrived, was that we should get a drink at the end of the day. I told him that I had plans." She shrugged and pulled her arm to one side, stretching barely used muscles. "*These* are my plans."

Naya and Ella shared a glance, and shuddered with revulsion. "He is such a slime ball," Cassy grumbled to no one in particular, staring straight ahead even though the aerobics instructor was still sifting through her music near the sound system.

Naya had to agree, having heard about Darren before. He was a sexual harassment lawsuit just waiting to happen. "Yeah, be careful around him. He's slimy and skeevy, who knows what he'd do."

Cassy clenched her teeth. She didn't want to repeat Darren's other comments after the lunch break. She needed to think about what Darren had said and talk herself back from the brink of fury. She needed to calm herself down and bury all of her hurt and anger because it wasn't productive. Men like Darren were slime. Nothing more.

Cassy thought about telling Naya and Ella about Mr. Ferocious. But for some reason, she couldn't do it. Was it...perhaps...that her conversations with the man were...maybe a little special? Special and personal?

Good grief! What was she thinking? Her interactions with the man hadn't been special! They'd been...nerve-wracking!

Cassy shook her head. "You are in *so* much trouble," she muttered to herself.

Instead of lingering on the exciting sensation of talking with the tall, dangerous man, Cassy focused on Darren's obnoxiousness. Turning, she watched Ella and Naya stretching, preparing for the aerobics class.

With a huff, she grumbled, "It isn't fair that he gets to make the female population miserable simply because he's closer to becoming a partner."

Ella and Naya smiled, glancing at Cassy, who had already staked out her position on the hardwood floor, obviously eager for the class to start. "Yeah. I think someone should do something about that," Ella said pointedly, raising her eyebrows.

Cassy would have said something more, but the aerobics instructor slipped her microphone over her head and called everyone to get rowdy, trying to pep up the class participants. The three of them lined up among the other participants as class started.

Fifty-five minutes later, Ella and Cassy stumbled after Naya as they headed out.

Naya bounced, energized after class, while Ella and Cassy lurched as best they could down the street. Ella and Naya didn't work close by, but they'd driven to Cassy's building and parked because it was the garage closest to the gym.

"See you guys!" Naya called, waving as she headed for her car.

Cassy stood by her own car, sweat still soaking her shirt as she stared at the door handle, wondering if she had the strength to get in.

"You okay?" Ella asked, heading towards her own car, which was parked a few spaces away.

Cassy stood there staring at the door, barely able to nod her head.

Ella walked slowly over to her friend, also staring at the door handle. "Why aren't you getting into your car?" she asked.

Cassy stared at the door for another long moment, willing the door to open on its own. Unfortunately, it didn't comply. Darn shame, she thought as she sighed. "I can't lift my arms," she admitted.

Ella laughed weakly. "I was afraid you were going to say that. I was going to ask you for a ride because I can't lift mine either."

The two women nodded to Naya as she drove out of the parking lot, looking completely refreshed and revived. "Why do we let her drag us to these classes?" Cassy asked.

Ella chuckled. "I think you chose this one, my friend."

Cassy grunted, her only indication that she disagreed. "Well, next class, I'm going to watch you guys while drinking one of those strawberry smoothies while sitting against the wall."

Ella laughed again, her head falling backwards because it was too hard to hold her head up and laugh at the same time. "No, you won't. You're the most irritatingly optimistic of all three of us. By the next time we decide to take a class, you will be fully recovered and think you can make it through the class with more energy. You'll also convince yourself that we'll have lithe, sexy bodies by the end of class. But in reality, Naya is the only one that will look good. Those curves don't need exercise to look amazing."

Cassy snorted as she took in her friend's full breasts, tiny waist, and long, slender legs. "Yeah. You're clearly the ugly duckling of the group."

"Shut up and figure out how to unlock your door. You can drive me to my car."

Cassy grunted again. "Your car is parked three spaces down from mine."

Ella glanced over her shoulder and shook her head. "I won't make it."

The two found themselves holding each other up as they giggled, knowing that somehow, one of them would need to find the strength to open their car door. Cassy sighed and pushed her still sweaty hair out of her eyes. "Okay, time to go home and work now. I was stuck in a meeting *all* day today and now I have to get caught up on everything I couldn't do during the day." She felt her phone vibrate in her tote bag, indicating that she had yet another e-mail to deal with.

Ella shook her head. "You're going to burn out if you keep doing twenty hour days, Cassy." She pushed away from her friend's car, forcing her feet to carry her towards her own.

Cassy waved weakly as they departed.

Fifteen minutes later, she unlocked the door to her apartment, her arms still weak and her muscles protesting, but there was nothing wrong with her body that a good pizza couldn't fix, she thought. And a beer. Did she have any beer left? She wasn't sure. Maybe there was some wine leftover from the other night when Ella and Naya had been over. They had been commiserating about their love lives. Well, their *lack* of love lives, she corrected as she pushed her key into the lock of her apartment door.

Her stomach grumbled and she wondered how long it would take for the pizza to be delivered. Probably too long. Maybe she would soak in a bubble bath and relax. Even dialing the phone seemed like too much hassle.

She tossed her keys onto the kitchen counter as she passed by, dumping her computer case and gym bag, now filled with her work clothes, on the floor.

She was just about to enter her bedroom when movement to her right caught her eye. She glanced over, just in time to see a shadowy figure stand up. Her scream as the large form approached should have alerted the police three blocks away. She wasn't sure how her neighbors could have missed it. It also had the galvanizing effect of shooting adrenaline through her system. Since flight wasn't a possibility, she took a fighting stance, more than ready to defend her honor and her furniture.

"Get out!" she screeched, her hands already in position.

The raspy chuckle startled her. Did rapists and burglars laugh? And did they always sound so...sexy?

"Relax, little one," the voice murmured. A light flipped on and she blinked. "Nasir," she whispered, stunned and terrified for a whole slew of different reasons now. Then she shook her head, closing her eyes as she frantically tried to remember how Darren had addressed him. "I mean, Your Highness!"

She looked around, feeling vulnerable in her skimpy workout clothes that were sticky with sweat. Her hair was matted to her head and she was pretty sure that her makeup had been either sweated or wiped off. She tried to tug her top down lower, wishing it was long enough to hide her stomach and Cassy vehemently prayed that she didn't have mascara streaks on her cheeks.

Goodness, he was so sophisticated and gorgeous, but not in a traditional way. No, he could never be classified as classically handsome. Not even close. He was rugged, raw, dangerous. Terrifying. Why did that word keep popping up in reference to this man? Why couldn't she come up with another adjective?

Because it was perfect to describe him.

"What are you doing here? And how did you get into my apartment?" She should be nervous, shouldn't she? Well, she *was* nervous. The man was huge and there was something about him that just...set off her nerves. But she didn't feel like she was in danger. At least not physical danger.

His dark eyes moved over her features and Cassy again felt the need to wipe under her eyes, just in case her mascara was smudged.

Lifting his hands in the air, he nodded at her nervousness. "I'm truly sorry to have invaded your privacy, Cassandra. I saw the way your co-worker looked at you after our lunch and I didn't want any other rumors to be applied to you. But I came to see you." He paused, letting his words sink in. "We didn't have enough time to talk after lunch today." His eyes surveyed her figure in the revealing clothes. "I would like to have dinner with you, if that is convenient," he explained.

Cassy froze. Was he serious? What was going through his mind? Seriously?

Somewhat flattered and...okay, so she was impressed that he'd been so considerate. Not many men would have noticed another man being sexually rude. So the fact that Nasir had noticed Darren's rudeness earlier was...interesting. Still, Cassy couldn't let this man into her life.

She crossed her arms over her chest, feeling naked with those dark eyes on her. She shook her head, feeling her wet hair stick to the nape of her neck and wishing she had more clothes on. "No. But thank you for the invitation," she said with just enough bite that he couldn't miss, trying to come across as firm. She really should be upset that he'd broken into her apartment but...well, he had a valid reason. And in truth, she was grateful that he'd been so considerate.

Thankfully, the black eyebrow that lifted appeared more amused than offended. Unfortunately, his reaction didn't bode well for her getting him out of her apartment quickly. Goodness, she was in a pickle here. How does one tell off one of the most important clients she'd ever had?

"It looks like you had quite the workout. I'm sure you are ravenously hungry."

She opened her mouth to tell him that she wasn't hungry at all, but her stomach chose that moment to grumble loudly. "I am hungry. So, if you would be so kind," she emphasized the last word, "get *out* of my apartment, then I can shower and have my dinner."

He reached out, gently caressing her arm, setting her skin on fire. And a whole bunch of other things, she realized, praying that he wouldn't notice that her nipples were pressed against the thin material of her exercise top.

Had his eyes flickered downwards? She wasn't sure, but she'd wager her next paycheck that they had.

But he was also relentless. "Tonight you are tired and I invaded your privacy. Eventually, you will trust me. At that point, we will dine together and you will tell me all about yourself and your friends. I'm truly fascinated and interested to know all about you."

She couldn't believe his...it wasn't exactly arrogance since the guy was actually apologizing. But...! Cassy clung to her anger, even though she wasn't sure that she had a reason for it any longer. He'd apologized twice for invading her privacy, plus he had a valid reason.

Still, he wasn't the kind of man she normally dated. Deep down inside, Cassy knew that she wouldn't ever be able to control this man. And Cassy always needed control when she dated any man.

Stiffening her shoulders, she looked up at him. "No," she replied firmly, shifting her feet so that she was better balanced. "I'm going to shower and have dinner all by myself and work for the rest of the evening. If you have something you need, then you should call my office."

Nasir almost laughed, delighted with her spunk. Other women would be throwing themselves at him by now. They would also already be naked, most likely. But this little beauty was shaking in her shoes, while looking sexy as hell. "I'm truly sorry to have scared you, Cassandra," he offered quietly, his eyes moving over her features. "But we will be together. There is something undeniable between us," he said, moving slightly closer.

She tried to back up, to make some space. But her feet wouldn't move. The wall behind her didn't help either. She shivered when his hand came up to touch her jaw, caressing her in a way that no man had ever taken the time to do. Most men were after just one thing and it frightened her that this man was approaching her in a different manner. She understood the male species only on one level – the boorish one. This simple, gentle caress left her breathless not to mention confused and... wanting more? Surely not!

"I don't play games," she finally managed to say even though her lips felt numb.

He looked down at her from his great height for another long moment and she held her breath, praying he would go away. This was not a man she could handle! He terrified her and made her feel things that she didn't like, let alone understand.

"Understood," he said, nodding his head. "You have set the rules and I will follow them." He let his hand fall away from her cheek and Cassy was horrified to find herself wishing he would continue touching her. "For now, little one. But be assured of one thing," he murmured, his eyes moving over her face. "You are an excellent lawyer, and a beautiful woman. I'd like to explore both of those parts of you." Another soft caress that caused her heart to skip a beat...well...several beats, actually.

A moment later, he was gone. Cassy touched the place where his finger had set her skin on fire, blinking to try to focus on reality. It was hard because a small part of her wanted to race towards the door where he'd just disappeared and beg him to stay. Their conversation over lunch this afternoon had been...stimulating!

But that was silly, she told herself. She couldn't actually WANT to spend time with that man! No, she was just tired –exhausted actually– after a long night working and then a grueling workout.

That must be it, she thought. She was just losing her mind. Cassy sighed, telling herself that exhaustion was the only answer as to why she would want that man to come back.

With a sigh, she picked up her phone and ordered her pizza. "Better make it a large tonight," she told the operator at her favorite pizza parlor. She didn't even cringe at the extra calories. She couldn't eat the whole pizza tonight, but she looked forward to having her dinner already made for the next several nights! She'd eat an extra apple during the day, she promised herself. And a banana.

Okay, so she wasn't going to do either of those. Nor was she going to make herself a salad, which might dilute some of the grease.

Cassy walked over to her fridge and peered inside. No salad. Actually, no food at all. She had a single, small cup of yogurt, but other than that....

Slamming the fridge closed, she walked away, feeling righteous because she'd at least attempted to have a salad, then jumped into the shower, quickly washing off the sweat and stress of the day. When she was finished, she pulled on a pair of leggings and an old sweatshirt just in time for the doorbell to ring, indicating that her pizza had arrived.

For the next five hours, she ate pizza, sipped wine, and worked on the cases she'd ignored during the day. And if her thoughts lingered on a certain man with the most incredible shoulders and eyes that could melt her insides? Well, she just told herself to focus harder! Nobody was going to stop her from making partner!

Chapter 2

"You're on a flight to Zurich," Darren announced as he poked his head into Cassy's doorway.

Cassy looked up, startled by both his sudden appearance as well as his words. But by the time she was able to focus on something other than her computer monitor, he was already gone, leaving her baffled, wondering if she'd heard him correctly. "I'm what?" she asked in confusion. But neither the screen in front of her nor the case file beside her were willing to explain. Standing up, Cassy hurried down the hallway, trying to catch up with the guy.

"Darren!" she called out. He slowed, glancing over his shoulder at her. "What did you just say?" she asked, coming to a stop, more than a little breathless. The occasional aerobics class wasn't really helping her cardiovascular system when she ate several slices of pizza afterwards.

Darren kept walking as he said, "You're needed in Zurich. We are in charge of overseeing the transfer of a house." He shrugged a shoulder dismissively. "It might actually be a palace or something like that."

Cassy blinked, then stopped, not sure if she'd understood correctly. Going to Zurich was one thing. But she was supposed to help with the sale of a palace? Really? Surely, she'd misunderstood. When she realized that she was standing in the hallway, alone once again, she hurried after Darren who had made it almost to his office. "One of our clients owns *a palace*?"

Darren scowled at her. "Weren't you listening?" He glanced impatiently at his watch. "You have less than an hour to get to the airport. Your flight takes off from Heathrow in about forty minutes."

Cassy gasped and checked the clock on the wall behind him. "I can't make it out to Heathrow Airport in forty minutes," she argued. "That's at least an hour's drive from here! Traffic will be a nightmare." She paused, thought about it, and corrected her statement. "Traffic is always a nightmare! No one could drive from downtown London to Heathrow airport in forty minutes!"

Darren had no compassion for a junior associate getting such a prime assignment. In fact, he was pissed that he hadn't been chosen, so he took his irritation out on Cassy. It sounded like a peach assignment. He'd love to take over the task, go through the contracts, and ensure that all of the signatures were done correctly. He would then take in the night life, hit one of the nicer restaurants in the downtown Zurich area, relax for a couple of days, and charge everything to the client.

But this particular client had specifically asked for Cassy, which meant she would get additional visibility with the senior level partners and that meant she was that much closer to making partner. That meant she'd make it to partner level two years earlier than he'd made partner. And that simply wasn't going to work. No, he wanted the oh-so-ador-ably-sexy Cassandra Flemming in his bed, not in the boardroom with him.

He snidely turned to glare down at her. "You can make it to the air-port if you hurry. A car should be waiting for you downstairs." After slamming her, and making sure that other associates overheard his deri-sion, he continued on his way, ignoring the sputtering woman who was trying to figure things out. He definitely wasn't going to help her. She could figure things out for herself, since she was so damn smart!

Cassy stared after him for a long moment, still not sure what was going on. Refusing to back down, she followed Darren into his office. "Darren, I don't even have clothes packed. What's this all about?"

Darren picked up several case files and his jacket, then looked at her with exasperation and impatience. "Look, Cassy. You're needed in Zurich. Your assistant has all the details. I would be going myself," he lied and added a bit more bite to his tone, "but I have court in fifteen minutes. So get your ass downstairs and get to the airport. If you have any questions, ask your damn assistant."

And with that, he walked out the door, leaving Cassy to stare after him with her mouth hanging open. Zurich? A palace? Cassy thought the Queen of England was the only one that owned palaces. But what did she know? She was just a bourgeois lawyer trying to figure out which end was up.

As she left Darren's office, her assistant, Melanie, rushed up to her. "Finally! I've been looking everywhere for you!" She shoved a piece of paper in her hand. "I just got an e-mail about something that's go-ing on in Zurich. Here's the address where you'll be staying and the

23

information on your flight." She handed Cassy a file folder. "Here's the information on the property. No transfer of funds, it is a gift, but the legal international issues need to be reviewed before the transfer can take place."

Melanie handed Cassy her coat and her black tote bag. "I've rescheduled your meetings so your schedule is clear. I'll send you more information as soon as I can. But you have to hurry. There's a car downstairs waiting to take you to the airport. The driver's name is Tom and he's going to get you out to the airport on time."

"But what about my passport?"

Melanie tugged the black bag hanging over Cassy's shoulder and dropped something inside. "In your bag."

"And clothes?" she asked, still confused.

"A corporate credit card is in there as well."

Cassy peeked into her bag while hurrying down the hallway. She'd never seen her passport, never had a need for it before although the law firm required all of its lawyers to have one ready. Obviously for emergencies like this. And a corporate credit card? Weren't those used for things like office supplies? Surely she wasn't being given permission to buy clothes and toiletries on a corporate account!

Melanie pressed the button on the elevator while Cassy opened the file explaining the details and pictures of the house...er...palace. She could see why it was considered a palace! The house was incredible! Twelve thousand square feet, indoor pool, ten bedrooms...the list went on and on. "This is gorgeous!" she breathed, flipping through the pictures included in the file.

Melanie sighed. "Tell me about it. My little seven hundred square foot apartment could fit into one of those bathrooms."

Tom drove through the heavy afternoon traffic, heading west out of the city. Heading west on any highway at the end of the day was asking for a several-hour nightmare. Commuters were jockeying for position, cutting people off, drivers enduring complete stops for several minutes then some magical break occurred in the traffic which allowed everyone to go from a complete standstill to a wondrous five miles per hour, only to come to a standstill again, a half mile later.

Tom seemed to have a secret, mysterious way of getting around traffic. Of course, he avoided all the major highways, using back roads that Cassy had never even heard of before. He drove through neighborhoods with huge houses right next to small homes, then through commercial areas and more residential areas. Thirty five minutes after she stepped into the car, he turned onto the access road that would take them right up to the airport.

Cassy checked the time, shoulders tense as she watched the seconds tick by. "I'm still going to miss the flight, aren't I?" she asked, sitting on the edge of her seat and glancing through the windows, wondering how he got around the cars so fluidly.

"It won't leave without you," Tom assured her.

Cassy wondered how he could possibly know that as he drove past the main terminal and through a guarded gate. "What are you doing?" she asked. "Where are we going?"

Tom drove up to a large, private plane. "Why are we stopping here?" she asked, her nervousness increasing.

"This is your flight, ma'am," he explained with a quick glance in his rear-view mirror. As soon as he came to a stop, Tom jumped out of the car and held the back door open for her.

"I'll take her luggage," someone called, hurrying up to the town car.

Cassy stepped out and looked around, hoping that she didn't look like a bumpkin as she stared at the huge plane with a rolling staircase pushed up to the open door. A private plane? A flight to Zurich on a private plane? Was she dreaming? Cassy actually pinched herself, sure that she wasn't awake.

"Ma'am, do you have any luggage?" a worker in a navy uniform asked politely when she continued to stare at the private plane.

Someone touched her arm and she jumped. "Excuse me?" she asked of the man standing beside her.

"Do you have any luggage? The back of your vehicle was empty."

Luggage? Did she have luggage? The question pinged around her numb brain for several moments as she tried to process the question. Luggage. Clothes. Stuff she would need!

"No. No luggage," she explained. "I only learned that I was flying to Zurich less than an hour ago." She tried to pull herself together, shake herself out of her shock. "I believe this is just a quick trip." She missed the confusion on the worker's face as she headed for the stairs. Even as she climbed, Cassy looked around, a surreal sensation surrounding her.

"Good afternoon, Ms. Flemming," a flight attendant greeted Cassy as she stepped aboard. "We're ready for takeoff whenever you are."

Cassy nodded and sat down on one of the luxurious seats, feeling silly and self-conscious. When the flight attendant started to shut the plane door, Cassy sat up a bit, not sure what was going on. "Isn't anyone else taking this flight?" She'd never been on a private plane before so all of this was all new to her.

The flight attendant smiled and shook her head, carefully locking the door. "No ma'am. You are our only passenger." The pilot nodded brief-ly to Cassy after coming out of what was most likely the galley area and then settled into his seat, closing the cockpit door. The next thing she knew, the plane was speeding down the runway.

As soon as they were airborne, she tried to relax into the large, comfortable chair.

As much as she wanted to savor the unanticipated luxury of the flight, less than an hour into it, Cassy fell sound asleep. She hadn't been sleeping well so it was difficult to keep her eyes open as the airplane swept smoothly over Europe.

By the time the flight attendant gently woke her, the plane was preparing to land and it was close to twilight, Zurich time. Unfortunately, Cassy had only gotten about six hours of sleep over the past three days and she could barely keep her eyes open, even as the plane taxied to a stop. She vaguely remembered walking down the stairs of the plane and stepping into the back seat of another waiting town car, but she'd fallen back asleep snuggled into the soft leather seat.

Chapter 3

The softness of the bed called to her, tempting her to simply bury her face in the extremely soft pillow and ignore the world. She didn't want to wake up because she was warm, cozy, and felt better than she had in a long, long time. Cassy didn't want to let go of that feeling. So instead, she snuggled deeper into the blankets.

A knock on the door startled her and she automatically called out, "Come in!"

Sighing, she rolled over in the bed and...wait. Where was she?

Deep, husky laughter startled her awake. "You're not fully awake yet, are you?"

Her eyes popped open and she looked around, noticing for the first time that this wasn't her lumpy, ugly bed. The mattress was too soft and the pillows too wonderful. Also, there was no way she'd be able to afford sheets and a comforter of this quality.

Cassy's gaze landed on the man standing beside the bed. "What are you doing here?" she whispered, feeling disoriented, confused, and bedraggled next to his sophistication. And she wanted a toothbrush! Good grief, why was he in her hotel room?

"You invited me in?" he prompted, a teasing look in his dark, sexy eyes.

She sat up and looked around. This didn't look like any hotel room she'd ever stayed in, she thought, taking in the beautiful décor, the expensive furniture, and the gorgeous windows. And yellow? She wouldn't have thought that a hotel would decorate a room in yellow. That seemed very odd. Normally, hotels decorate in more neutral colors. Didn't they?

"What's going on?" She realized she was practically naked. She was still wearing her underwear and bra, but nothing else. Then she re-

27

membered being led up into this room by a smiling woman who had asked if she needed anything. Cassy had assured the woman, whoever she was, that she was fine. As soon as she'd been alone, Cassy had simply pulled off her clothes and gotten into bed, falling instantly into a dreamless sleep.

Nasir's dark eyes watched her as he leaned a muscular shoulder against the wall. When he spoke, she could tell that he was trying hard not to laugh. "You arrived at my home last night. My housekeeper told me this morning that you were beyond exhausted last night."

"Yes, but..." she pushed her hair out of her eyes. "Why am I here?"

He laughed softly. "I need your legal expertise. You're here to help me transfer my house as a gift to Mikal."

She blinked, her hand clutching the sheet to her chest. His presence, those bulging biceps in his arms and his long legs...they weren't helping her thinking process. "Who is Mikal?"

Nasir stepped closer, seeing small glimpses of her plain, cotton underthings and the idea that this beautiful woman wore only serviceable items seemed...well, that was an issue for later, he told himself.

Obviously, she'd been working too hard, pushing herself to exhaustion. Otherwise, she never would have taken her clothes off last night and simply dumped them beside the bed.

As she shifted on the bed, his eyes noticed something horrific. The woman wore a sports bra! It was such a crime to contain those beautiful breasts in a sports bra. As a man, he was offended. As her future lover, he was determined. A sports bra? Underneath a business suit? That could not be allowed. She should be draped in beautiful things, lacy intimates, as well as silks and satins.

And yet, Nasir couldn't seem to pull his fascinated gaze away from her delectable body. He wouldn't touch her at the moment, but she was delectably tempting with her cheeks still rosy from sleep. But Nasir preferred his lovers awake and participative versus barely conscious.

Still, he wasn't blind! And the image of those serviceable, practical underthings just...he was offended on her behalf.

"Why do you wear a sports bra under your suits?" he asked, reaching out to push a lock of dark hair out of her eyes. She looked soft, warm, and incredibly inviting just now. It was taking all of his control to not pull that sheet back and make love to her. The spark that he'd noticed in the meeting had only grown stronger, but instead of fanning the flames of that spark, Nasir resisted, wanting...more. He wanted to... understand her. Which was completely out of character for him. Usually, he preferred his mistresses uncomplicated. So what was the allure

28

Cassandra held for him?

Cassy bit her lower lip, trying to remain sophisticated but feeling completely inadequate. Tucking her legs up underneath her, even though the fluffy comforter was still covering her, she looked around. "Um... where are my clothes?"

"My housekeeper picked them up earlier this morning when she tried to wake you up." He moved over to the wall where apparently a coffee service had been rolled in. "Cream, no sugar, right?" he asked, looking at her over his shoulder.

Cassy pushed her hair out of her eyes, hoping to look presentable but she suspected that she had mascara smudges under her eyes, no doubt her lipstick was completely gone, and her hair probably resembled a rat's nest at this point. Traveling was not kind to one's appearance, even in a private plane.

That's when her eyes and brain surged into action, registering the delicate china cup in his hands. Coffee! Goodness, the moment she realized it was here, the fabulous scent hit her and she nodded eagerly. "Yes. Thank you." Why was she being so polite? Shouldn't she be screaming and demanding answers? And dressing?!

She felt completely off kilter and he was acting as if everything going on, including her being almost naked, were completely normal events in the course of his day. "Um...where did she take them?"

Why did his lack of concern for her near-naked state irritate her? He was almost blasé about her lack of clothing. She shouldn't care that this man was used to naked women lounging around. It shouldn't bother her because it was none of her business. He was a business client. Nothing else.

Okay, so her gaze roamed up and down his legs...uh, okay, honestly... she was looking at his tight butt. She shouldn't be looking at a client's butt. She shouldn't even be *thinking* about a client's butt, much less admiring said client's butt while telling herself that he had a nice butt. Nope, butt admiration was not part of her law firm's services!

When he turned around, one dark eyebrow went up and she knew it was because her cheeks were turning red. Cassy tried to play it off, pretend she was sophisticated and all of this...craziness...was totally normal. But it was hard because...well, he was gorgeous and scary and terrifying and had muscles that she'd like to...!

Nope! *Client*, she reminded herself firmly. And a client who was in her bedroom and...! Not good! Cassy should *not* be thinking of stripping Nasir naked! Clients and clothes-taking-off were a bad combination, one that could potentially get her fired, even if the idea sent a

29

delicious shiver through her.

He brought a cup of coffee to her and Cassy carefully accepted it, hold-ing the sheet in front of her with her other hand.

"Your business suit was sent to the dry cleaners. And I'll probably have a tailor fix it. The cut and style are completely wrong for you."

Cassy had just taken a sip of her coffee but his words made her choke.

He waited patiently until she'd gotten her breath back. "Wrong *cut?*" She frowned up at him for a moment, not really understanding. Her suit was a good suit! She'd gotten it on sale at one of the better depart-ment stores, so she knew there wasn't anything wrong with it. Still, she couldn't stop the question, "What do you mean?"

He sat down in a chair beside the bed, his own cup of coffee in his hands. "Which statement confused you?"

Cassy stared down at the comforter, not sure which question needed an answer more quickly. "I guess I'd like to know why you took my clothes to the dry cleaners without permission. I wasn't told about this trip until literally the last minute, so I wasn't given time to head home and pack." she explained. Then looked up at him, pleading for under-standing. "I don't have anything else to wear!"

Instead of reacting to her indignant answer, his eyes heated up. Previ-ously, his gaze had focused on her face but with her question, his eyes traveled downward, noticing the curves under the covers. "I think I'm in a better position than I thought earlier today."

Oh goodness, his voice had become deeper. Sexier! Cassy felt her toes curl with excitement!

"Because I don't have any clothes?" she asked, stunned, furious, and trying to ignore that anticipation curling inside of her.

"Exactly." When his eyes moved back to hers, she stopped breathing for a moment.

Clearing her throat and pushing those delicious thoughts away, Cassy reminded herself that she was his lawyer. "This isn't appropriate *at all*, Your Highness."

That irritating amusement was back in his dark, enigmatic eyes. "Since I am going to make love to you by the end of the day, perhaps it would be more appropriate for you to call me Nasir."

For a long moment, she stared up at him, her mind filled with images of his big hands against her skin, his mouth kissing hers, and all sorts of erotic, wonderful and...Cassy sputtered, shocked both by her imagina-tion as well his arrogance. "I'm not...!" She tried to finish the sentence but it was lost with the horror, and secret excitement, of what he was suggesting. "We're not..."

"I assure you, we are."

Unfortunately, a different pair of eyes popped into her mind. Eyes that weren't promising heaven – but had thrown her into a daily hell. A hell she hadn't thought about in a long time. The memory caused her to shrink, cringing with long-dormant pain.

Those memories were exactly what she needed to get her mind back on track.

With a defiant lift of her chin, Cassy shook her head adamantly. "You don't understand. Both scenarios are impossible." She shifted on the bed, setting the coffee cup on the table beside her, trying to appear professional, but that was difficult to pull off when she was nearly naked. "Now, if you would just give me back my clothes, I'll do the work you hired my firm to do, and will be out of your way."

Nasir waited until she'd set her coffee cup back down before he touched her. With a gentleness that was startling in such a large man, he loomed over her, his hands moving softly over her face before sliding down her arm to send tingles of pleasure through her body. The sensation was so startling, she shifted uncomfortably on the bed.

But she didn't try to get away from his touch. In fact, her arms shifted slightly, inadvertently asking for more. It was so staggering, the way this simple touch made her feel, that she looked down at his hand, then back up to his eyes. All memories of that malicious memory of so long ago vanished from her mind as his fingers tenderly stroked her skin, sending shivers of fire down her spine.

She wanted answers, but the heat in those dark eyes didn't give her any information. No, those eyes were only promising more of the same and she wasn't sure she could handle more.

His fingers tangled with hers and he turned her hand over, his rough thumb swirling patterns on a patch of skin that she'd never known could be an erogenous zone until this moment. It was so surprising that she couldn't stop her toes from curling, startled by the sensations that were making her insides melt with desire. A completely inappropriate desire!

"I think you need to understand something, my beauty," he murmured, his fingers still caressing her arm. "I would like to make love to you by the end of this day. I would also enjoy getting to know you a little better because I sense a softness within you, a vulnerability that I like and do not want to destroy. But I feel a need in you and you can rest assured that it is just as strong in me. So, don't doubt that we are going to explore this together." He paused, his eyes taking in her soft mouth, her vulnerable, dark eyes and he leaned back slightly. "The last time we were together, I could feel your eyes on me when you thought I wasn't looking, felt the burning when we touched. Please, Cassandra, give us this time to explore this together."

She wanted to tell him to go to hell. Instead, her body tensed, waiting for more of his touch. The ice around her heart that had hardened all those years ago, melted slightly when he told her that he sensed her vulnerability. At the same time, her stomach quivered with the shame from those memories from so long ago and a deep ache that had never fully healed. She'd been wounded by harsh, insensitive words and a terrifying moment. That feminine side of her, the part that might have agreed to his suggestion...she'd hidden that part of herself for too long.

"I can't," she whispered, even while her hands curled into fists to keep herself from reaching out to touch him. "I can't do any of that." Why was she pleading with him? Why was she so desperate for him to understand? What power did he have over her that she couldn't just slap his face and demand that he leave her alone?

His eyes searched hers, moving downwards, noticing the abhorrent sports bra that flattened her full, ripe breasts against her chest. Cassy tried to hide her body's reaction, but her breathing was labored as she fought to control her need.

"You feel it, don't you?" he asked gently.

She almost cried out when his hands smoothed against her fingers, causing her fingers to release the tight grip she had on the comforter. She wanted to tell him why she needed to maintain that hold, because otherwise, she was afraid her hands might...they would...touch him, explore him. That *could not happen*!

But even as she thought that, her back arched slightly, feeling his breath against her neck. "Please," she told him. Although Cassy wasn't sure if she was begging him to stop or to give her more of those delicious, fluttering kisses along her neck.

Never had she felt this way towards a man. She'd thought she'd shut down that part of herself. So long ago, as her body had matured, the boys had definitely noticed. The names the others had called her had hurt deeply. She'd learned to suppress this need, to ignore all of her desires because everyone considered her to be a bad person. In her mind, everything about sexuality was wrong and sinful. She'd endured too many hours of taunting, too many cruel comments from her classmates, to think anything else.

And now this man, with the challenge and the lust in his eyes, was bringing all of that back. He was showing her that she was a woman again.

Suddenly, instead of the passion of moments before, those horrible memories surfaced and she pulled back, her eyes startled, horrified that she could...that she might want to...!

All of the unpleasant memories came rushing back. The embarrassing way her body swayed when she moved without the tight sports bra. Or the way the boys in high school had watched her breasts with salacious glee while the girls in school had looked on with malevolent fury even as Cassy had pressed her books against her chest, trying to hide her figure. Nothing had worked. They'd still stared and, to this day, Cassy was self-conscious of her breasts. And now, she was painfully embarrassed at the way he could make her feel, of the thoughts surging through her mind, and the need making her body feel things that were...wrong.

"Please," she whispered again, but this time, it wasn't a plea for him to continue. This time, it was a plea to stop. Cassy closed her eyes as that dreadful need almost choked her.

Pushing off the bed, he looked down at her and Cassy was painfully aware of her awkward position, curled up on the enormous bed, nearly naked and completely defenseless. She pulled the sheet higher to cover herself, her only defense against those vicious memories and her current shame that her body would betray her in such a way. Relieved, she lifted her eyes, looking right back at him with gratitude that he hadn't pushed her further.

Nasir saw that shame and knew that something had shifted inside of her. Something dark and he didn't like it. He stepped back again, giving her more space.

The legal side of Cassandra was a powerful woman. He'd watched her in the meeting back in London, repeatedly impressed with her knowledge of international law, the intricacies of various challenges. He's also appreciated her suggestions on how to overcome those challenges.

But now, seeing that haunted look in her eyes, Nasir knew that Cassandra was complicated. There was something holding her back. He had to respect that. He wanted to banish the bad memories and replace them with good ones, but before he could do that, he had to understand her.

"There are clothes in the closet for you," he said, his voice even huskier than before. "Take your time getting ready and join me downstairs. We will meet in a half hour."

Relief surged through Cassy. She watched as he walked away, distracted momentarily from her pain by the strength in his shoulders and arms. The sweater displayed his muscles better than the gorgeous suit he'd worn back in London and she didn't like that she noticed these details.

She pulled her eyes away as he walked out of the bedroom, closing the door behind him quietly.

Taking deep breaths, she tried to calm herself down, wanting to be professional and sophisticated but knowing that she'd destroyed that image completely with her panic a few moments ago.

She didn't laugh at the "take your time" in one breath followed by a time limit with his next words. Normally, a contradiction like that would amuse her but right now, she was too nervous and too confused by her reaction to his presence and his touch to find humor in anything.

Using the techniques she'd learned as a teenager to tune out the cruelly taunting memories, she eventually calmed her racing heart. It was tenuous, but eventually, she found her balance again.

Dragging her legs over the side of the bed, she wrapped the sheet around herself toga style. Peering into the closet, she found a complete wardrobe that included jeans, sweaters, tops, suits, even dresses. What in the world? All of the clothes still had tags on them, but no prices. That was curious.

Ignoring the clothes, she shook her head as she moved to the shower, wishing she could understand this man. He was so out of her league! Why was he even interested in her? He had to have women throwing themselves at him all the time. Why would he waste his time on a woman who had a screw loose because of a ridiculous childhood trauma that she should have gotten over a long time ago?

She dated nice, comfortable men. Perhaps they were a little bit... wimpy. But those were the types of men that she preferred. They were safer, she told herself as she used the peaches and cream shampoo on her hair, relaxing as the scent surrounded her and she diligently tried to wash away the fatigue and confusion.

After drying off, she stepped out of the bathroom and looked around nervously, anxious that Nasir would return uninvited. She didn't want to risk it, so she grabbed a pair of jeans and the first sweater that she touched, not even bothering to see if she liked the color and style or not. Cassy didn't care if she looked good or if the color was hideous with her skin tone. She was getting out of this place and finding a hotel room where she could put a bit of space between herself and the man that stirred unwanted sensations. Sure, that was a cowardly reaction. But Cassy didn't care. Not a whit! She was strong and competent all the time. This, she told herself, was a perfect day to retreat!

She'd learned the hard way that respect was the most important thing in a person's life. She thought about that for a moment, pulling a tube of lipstick out of her purse. Perhaps chocolate might rank higher, she corrected as she carefully applied the cheerful color. Or maybe a close second. Actually, the respect vs. chocolate ranking - that was a moment by moment issue, she decided.

Rolling her eyes and tossing the jeans and sweater onto the bed, Cassy hunted through the drawers, hoping to find underwear. Of course, when she finally found a pair of panties, she was struck dumb by the lacy things that he thought would pass for underwear. Holding up a delicate scrap by one finger, she stared at it, not even sure how to put it on. This lace...it looked...complicated!

Tossing the...whatever...back into the drawer, she picked up another. And another and another until she came up with something that looked like it might actually cover her bottom more thoroughly. Those thong things?! Nope! There's no way those could be comfortable. And anyone who tried to convince her that they could be was obviously lying!

The underwear she'd chosen looked decadent. And when she pulled it on, she actually turned to look at herself from behind in the mirror, startled by how her body looked. Especially her butt! "Wow!" she whispered.

"I agree," a deep voice said from the doorway.

Cassy spun around, grabbing the jeans from the bed and holding them in front of her like a shield. "What do you think you're doing?" she demanded furiously, her face turning a painful shade of red. "Get *out!*"

Nasir chuckled and moved closer, surveying her adorable backside in the mirror behind her that she'd obviously forgotten about. "The matching bra would look even more amazing on you," he suggested. He saw the shift in her breathing, the way her eyes changed, and the subtle but oh-so-delicious change in her body language. Yes, she was affected. Embarrassed, confused, and innocent, but still affected. She didn't want to be, which was a curiosity, but he would figure out why eventually. He was good at eliminating obstacles.

He sifted through the dozens of bras and lifted out the one that matched her underwear. The whole time, Cassy sputtered with outrage.

"Here," he urged. "Wear the matching bra and I'll meet you downstairs for lunch."

She grabbed the scrap of material that was dangling from his fingers and glared at him. "Just get out!" she hissed, only to receive an amused chuckle in response.

"As you wish," he finally said.

When the door closed, thankfully with him on the other side, she huffed as she tossed the tiny bra away. There was no way a bra like that could hold her in comfortably. She was too big-breasted to deal with a stupid scrap of lace like that. She grabbed her sports bra and snapped it into place, feeling better now that she was adequately covered, pulled in, and no jiggling could possibly take place. Not with this puppy, she thought grimly, pulling the sweater over her head.

Finally dressed, Cassy squared her shoulders as she pulled open the door. She'd show him choices, she thought furiously.

"Where is he?" Cassy demanded of a passing servant when she reached the bottom of an enormous, curving staircase. She refused to be intimidated by the staff members rushing around or the gigantic, crystal chandelier that hung in the foyer. A foyer that was too huge for any reasonable person. This entire home was too big and ostentatious! It screamed wealth and elegance, but seriously, why did one person need this much space and this many staff members?! It was ridiculous and only fueled her anger, giving her another reason for hating the man, other than the fact that he could make her want things that she didn't want to want.

The servant jumped in surprise and Cassy took a deep breath. "I apologize," she said with a calm she didn't feel, trying to force a smile but, going by the new expression on the servant's face, her smile was more ferocious than Cassy had intended. "I'm trying to find His Highness. Can you point me in the right direction?" she asked.

The servant was still wary and pointed to the left. "He's in the dining room, ma'am," she said, backing up a step.

"Thank you very much," Cassy replied, trying for a calm, professional expression.

Turning in the direction indicated, Cassy pushed open the doors, ignoring the two guards that were standing sentry outside the room. When she saw her target sitting at an intimate looking table, casually reading a newspaper, her temper flared. She fought to keep her temper under control, but he'd invaded her space without any sort of apology. And she suspected that he'd manipulated this whole trip to Zurich just to get to her.

"I will shoot you if you don't..." she didn't get a chance to finish. The two men who had been standing guard immediately grabbed her arms. An abrupt command halted their actions.

"What...?!" she gasped. She was released and Cassy turned, glaring at the two guards who were moving back reluctantly. Both still tense and ready to tackle her to the ground.

That's when she realized what she'd just said, or more specifically, threatened. One didn't voice a threat to shoot a man of Nasir's position and authority! "Sorry," she muttered with increasing irritation laced with contrition. "Bad choice of words."

Nasir laughed softly as he moved closer. "Cassy, do you even know how to shoot a gun?" he asked.

He was on his feet, towering over her. Waiting for an answer.

Unnerved, Cassy shifted on her feet nervously. He'd completely called her bluff, ignoring the point of the threat. "Well, no. Not really," she finally replied, crossing her arms over her breasts and glaring up at him defiantly.

Nasir chuckled and reached around her, putting a hand to the small of her back to lead her over to the table. "We'll have to fix that," he pulled out a chair for her.

"Fix what?" she asked, staring at all the food as her stomach grumbled with hunger. She suddenly realized how famished she was. Cassy had skipped both lunch and dinner the previous day, apparently having slept through both meals because of time zone changes and exhaustion.

"I will teach you how to shoot," he explained.

Cassy's mouth fell open. She wondered if he was making fun of her. But the serious expression told her that he wasn't. "Why would you offer to teach me how to shoot a gun?" she asked, her tone softening. No man had ever offered to help her before. Well, except her father. He'd been her main champion, her cheerleader, and the shoulder she'd cried on when the vicious taunts became too much.

Why would he, this powerful, intimidating, and most-likely horrendously busy man, offer to teach her anything? Much less teach her how to shoot moments after she'd just threatened to shoot him? A threat she was ashamed of now. Violence was never the answer and she shouldn't have even thought it, much less said it out loud.

What was it about this man that continuously threw her off guard? Most men were too busy trying to get her into bed. None had ever offered to help her with anything.

Granted, something about him told her that he wasn't the same as the men in her past. She couldn't quite define it, but he was...different. Definitely more powerful, but that wasn't exactly what was bothering her so profoundly.

Of course, his physical appearance was dramatically different from all the men she'd known. In her experience, men like Nasir were portrayed as killers, bad boys. But even so, as she watched him across the table as he conversed with someone who had brought him a report, there was something different about him. It was definitely the aura of power that surrounded him. But more than that. There was a harshness that he wore, almost like a protective barrier. Or maybe she was just romanticizing his persona in order to protect herself.

When the aide disappeared, he looked up as he sipped his coffee. "Did you have a good flight?" he asked.

A servant appeared with a silver coffee urn and poured her a cup of coffee. Cassy waited impatiently until they were alone again, not bothering to answer his question. She doubted he cared one way or another. And besides, she'd slept almost the entire trip. She remembered the takeoff and landing. Other than that, the flight was a blur.

"Why would you offer to teach me how to shoot?" she repeated.

Nasir looked at the lovely woman over the rim of his coffee cup, trying to understand her. She was a beautiful woman with a figure that could be extraordinary, if she would just eliminate that horrendous sports bra that she'd put back on instead of the pretty lace bra he'd suggested.

And why was she so skeptical of his offer? It wasn't just the offer to teach her how to shoot a weapon. He suspected that there was a much deeper question running through her subconscious.

He considered the various ways he could answer and reassure her. Nasir could tell her the truth, that she would need to know how to defend herself in the event that she needed to protect herself. In the time since he'd left her in the guest bedroom, he'd decided that he wanted Cassandra to be his wife, but he knew she wasn't ready to hear that. Besides, he didn't want to worry her. Not at this stage.

He wasn't going to explain that to her though. He didn't want his Cassy to be concerned about her safety.

Besides, he would protect his woman.

That didn't mean she shouldn't learn basic self-defense. Furthermore, from the background check his security team had done, he knew that she'd spent a great deal of time studying to become a lawyer and not enough time learning to be a woman.

So he went with a partial truth. "Because it would give me pleasure to teach you," he finally told her, thinking he sincerely would enjoy teaching her, seeing the joy of success in her pretty eyes. "We will start lessons after lunch. What would you like to eat?"

Cassy had no idea what was going on. Everything he said, she felt like there was a double meaning. But since she refused to let him get under her skin, she wasn't going to let him bother her. "I'll just have coffee," she told him. "And if you could bring me my bag, I can start working on the transfer of property for you. I understand that you're trying to sell this house?"

He shook his head. "We will do business later. Lunch first since you cannot function sufficiently on a cup of coffee." He pressed a button and a servant appeared behind him. "Ms. Flemming will have an omelet with everything," he told the woman who nodded and disappeared.

Cassy almost rolled her eyes, then turned to the servant. "Just ham and cheese, if you have it." The servant nodded, then turned to leave and Cassy faced Nasir once again. "You're awfully dictatorial," she told him, sipping the coffee in the hopes that the extra jolt might somehow help her make sense of this day. So far, everything was a confused jumble.

He laughed softly. "I have been accused of that many times in my lifetime." He shrugged. "I'm afraid that it comes with the job."

"Why did you break into my apartment last week?" she asked.

He shrugged. "Because I wanted to talk to you again. After the meeting at your office, you disappeared so quickly and I suspected that you didn't want your coworkers to notice our interest in each other. It seems that becoming intimately acquainted with a client would be frowned upon with your management. So, I was trying to be considerate." His eyes turned serious. "I'm truly sorry that I scared you. And I wasn't trying to invade your privacy, Cassandra. The opposite in fact. I was trying to ensure your privacy. That Darren fellow seemed to be particularly irritated that you answered more questions than he could, even though he was supposedly more experienced in international law." He paused before he said, "Not to mention, it is extremely difficult to have a private conversation for someone in my position. I took matters into my own hands and found a place where others would not intrude, nor would they even know about our conversation."

She could understand that. "But why break in?"

"Because I can," he teased, eager to see her eyes flash with anger again. He wasn't disappointed. He laughed before she spoke, interrupting her and diffusing her anger. "Actually, it was because I didn't want your employer to know about my interest in you. I didn't think it was any of their business. So, I thought it best not to have our dinner conversation overheard, or even known about, by the people in your firm. Dining in restaurants tends to bring out the photographers, so public dining wasn't an option either."

When he explained it in those terms, he seemed like a genuinely caring man!

She didn't want her law firm to know anything about her private life either, but that didn't mean she was willing to have a personal relationship with a client. That violated her personal ethics as well as her business code. Besides, the legal world was an ultra-conservative group in general, and those in London seemed to be particularly sensitive to gossip. There had been too many sex scandals in the legal community and her firm didn't want any dangerous gossip to poorly reflect upon their illustrious name or reputation.

"I see," she said softly, lowering her eyes. "But next time, how about calling my cell phone?"

He chuckled, the sound sending shivers throughout her body. "I will endeavor to be discreet without inciting your fears. Will that suffice?" he asked.

As a lawyer, Cassy knew that his response left open a wide range of possibilities. Even though she suspected it was a pretty major concession on his part, she couldn't let him get away with it. "Not really. I deserve to be treated with the same respect you deserve. And agreeing to 'not incite my fears' leaves a lot of violations of my privacy open to your dubious efforts at addressing my concerns."

He laughed again. "You are smart." Another aide walked in and whispered in his ear. Cassy tried to hide her exasperation at the repeated interruptions, but it was difficult. Whatever the aides were saying to him was obviously more important than their conversation, which made her feel unimportant.

Still, Cassy reminded herself that she was here as his legal representative. Her time was his and she needed to tamp down on her irritations and remain...professional wasn't the word she was looking for. Unflappable. Yes, that was the word. She needed to appear unflappable in Nasir's presence.

Whatever the aide said must have been agreeable because Nasir nodded sharply, signed the paper in front of him, and the aide quickly disappeared.

"Do they wake you when you're sleeping?" she asked, half sarcastically and half seriously. She wondered how the man lived with so many interruptions.

Nasir tilted his head slightly. "We are undergoing some delicate negotiations right now. I apologize for not giving you my full attention."

Cassy was irritated that he'd seen through her sarcasm. "I'm fine," she muttered, but inwardly, she was fuming.

His eyes lit up, sensing her anger. "You must be honest with me," he told her. "Otherwise, it will create difficulties in our relationship."

Cassy was so startled by his comment that she couldn't stop the burst of laughter. "Your Highness, we don't have a relationship, other than a professional one. I'm your lawyer and you are my client." She looked around, ignoring his arched eyebrow. "Now, if you could please get me my bag, we can discuss the issues surrounding the disbursement of this house." She paused for a moment. "It really is beautiful. If you don't mind me asking, why do you want to sell it?"

"I don't," he replied, shrugging one of those massive shoulders that so fascinated her. Eyes up, she reminded herself. Eyes off his shoulders.

Shoulders were not part of this transaction! Shoulders were nice...especially his shoulders...but shoulders didn't do business. Cassy castigated herself for allowing her eyes to move over his shoulders too many times.

How often had she been offended when a man couldn't keep his eyes off her breasts? There was no excuse for her doing the same to a man, no matter how deliciously broad and muscular his shoulders might seem.

She focused on his face. It took a long moment for his answer to sink in and when it finally did, Cassy was confused. "I thought I was here to help you sell this to one of your friends?"

Nasir took in the beautifully elegant room, almost as if he hadn't really looked at the house before this moment. "It was gifted to me several years ago. It has served its purpose. It is time for another purpose now."

She was amazed. Someone had given this house as a gift? Wow! Rich people really were different! "What purpose is it going to serve now?"

He shrugged and Cassy couldn't stop her eyes from dropping once again to those shoulders. They really were magnificent, she thought. But still...not her focus. Eyes up!

"It will be a gift. A gift of goodwill."

Cassy looked down into her coffee cup, not saying a word as she sifted through the legal implications of the transference of property. From his explanation, this transfer might be more complicated than she'd originally suspected. When she took a breath, she looked up at him. "Okay, so you're gifting this to a friend."

"Not a friend. At least, not a friend yet. I hope we will become friends eventually."

More confusion, but again, she pulled back all of her curiosity and focused on the task that her firm was hired to accomplish. "Gifting a house to another person still has tax ramifications. If you..."

"The financial issues will be dealt with by my accountants. I need you to draw up the papers that will transfer ownership. I need your expertise due to the transference of the property from one country, mine, to another country. There are many legal obstacles and you will be in charge of the language within the contract that will overcome those obstacles. The property taxes and insurance will be done through my accountants as well."

Cassy wasn't sure what to say, but her mind reeled with the huge responsibility. And yet, she couldn't relate to a world in which financial issues were cast aside. Income taxes, property taxes, insurance, and gifting of a house were...unheard of in her world.

A world she didn't understand and couldn't comprehend! It was so out of her realm! People from her sphere gifted a sweater or a tie. They didn't give someone else a house, much less a mansion in one of the priciest cities in the world.

She tried to hide her rural upbringing behind a façade of professionalism. "Understood, Your Highness."

"I gave you permission to call me Nasir," he pointed out.

Cassy shook her head, unaware of how her dark hair sparkled in the overhead lights. "I prefer to keep things professional, Your Highness."

He laughed softly. "Cassy, we will be so many things to each other in the future. You should learn that I don't take 'no' easily. You *will* call me by my first name, and accept that it will be your right."

She stiffened, although she wasn't sure about the meaning that seemed to be implied. So, instead of using his name or rejecting that "privilege," she moved on. "I can go down to the appropriate offices in town and file for a transfer of ownership. I just need to draw up the forms and confirm the clauses that would be necessary, set up the inspections, and put through the necessary documents to ensure a smooth transference of property rights. It shouldn't take long."

"You will stay here in Zurich as my guest for the next three days."

Cassy's mouth fell open. "But..."

"Three days, Cassandra," he interrupted firmly.

Cassy closed her mouth, her stubbornness rising up again. "It will take me less than a day to get all of the appropriate forms submitted and filed. I don't need three days. You can sign the papers tomorrow morning and, barring any problems with the property rights, this should be finished by tomorrow afternoon."

"Good," he said and the housekeeper stepped through the doorway with a covered dish that smelled divine. "Then we won't be bothered by business during the rest of our time together."

Cassy had no idea how to deal with this man. He was too confident, too powerful, and she was way out of her depth. Plus, this sexual tension was...she couldn't handle it.

Folding her hands together, she frowned at him. "I will leave here as soon as my work is finished," she replied firmly after a long silence. The housekeeper silently set the plate in front of her and removed the silver cover, then walked out of the room as silently as she'd entered.

Having unequivocally laid out her terms, Cassy couldn't resist digging into the perfectly cooked omelet. It had been a long time since anyone had cooked for her. She and her friends got together for dinner pretty often, but those meals were generally either pizza or Chinese takeout. So technically, someone else had cooked for her. But this meal was in a whole different category. Closing her eyes, she moaned at the delicious cheesiness. "Oh my!" she sighed with pleasure.

"I take it the omelet is good?"

Cassy looked up, her fork and a bite of the eggs and cheese frozen halfway to her mouth. It suddenly occurred to her that she had been scarfing the food down. She was acting as if she hadn't eaten in too long which, well, was true, but still...!

"I apologize," she lowered her fork. "What are you having to eat?"

He laughed again. "Please, continue. It's nice to see a woman eat something. Normally, women are too worried about gaining weight to actually enjoy the food."

Cassy's lips pressed together because she was one of those women. She'd love to lose another ten pounds but...she just loved eating too much. Besides, food was a stress outlet. Yes, she should learn to exercise in order to release the stress. But food...well, it tasted better. She enjoyed exercise sometimes, especially when Naya wasn't the one choosing the exercise class, but there was nothing better than a glass of wine, a pizza, and her friends to laugh away life's troubles.

"About this transference," she began.

"Please, finish your meal and we'll discuss business afterwards. You're obviously hungry."

She sighed and picked up her fork again. "You're a confusing man," she finally replied as she took another bite. The coffee was amazingly pungent with a strong flavor, the caffeine already hitting her from the cup he'd served her up in her bedroom.

And that brought up another issue. "About the sleeping arrangements," she said, trying to choose her words carefully.

"You will remain here, Cassandra."

Oh, that autocratic tone wasn't good for her stubborn, independent nature. "I don't think so," she told him. "It would be more appropriate if I were to stay in a hotel."

He chuckled, shaking his head. "I told you earlier that we will be lovers by the end of today. So, it's pointless for you to reserve a room at a hotel." He shook his head. "I don't think you could afford a hotel room in this part of Zurich anyway."

Her shoulders stiffened. "You don't know anything..." but she stopped at the look on his face. "The background check? The state of my bank account was included?"

Oh, that was embarrassing. She was a good lawyer, but she hadn't made partner yet. She was going to, she vowed. But until that happened, she wasn't making as much money as she eventually would earn. It was extremely expensive living in London. Her rent alone was

43

astronomical. Plus, there were her suits, which even though she bought them on sale, were still expensive. Not to mention buying matching shoes and her leather tote bag and a host of other expenses in order to maintain her professional appearance at the office.

"Of course your financials were included in the background check. My staff is quite thorough."

She sighed and rubbed her forehead, putting her fork down as her appetite dissipated. The idea of someone snooping through her life was... disconcerting.

"What else do you know about me?" she asked, her head bowed as she braced herself.

Nasir contemplated her body language and he didn't like it. Not one little bit. She was angry, but there was something more hidden behind those beautiful eyes. An edge that he couldn't quite figure out. She'd had that same look when she'd pulled away earlier today.

Instead of confronting her, he went on. "You graduated Magna Cum Laude from Georgetown University Law School, an impressive feat. Although you attended on a generous scholarship, you still have a hefty student loan to pay off, which you are doing with admirable regularity." She was still tense, as if waiting for him to say something horrible. "You have two very good friends whom you've known since your high school years. You're a social person at work, but you don't attend as many company functions as one might expect of a lawyer on the partner track. You have about two thousand dollars in your savings account, which would be higher but you're paying off those student loans at a faster rate than is strictly needed, especially taking into account the interest rate on those loans. Plus, you are also building up your professional wardrobe." Still no reaction, no movement. "You don't date, or you haven't in recent months...why is that?"

Cassy's head snapped up. "Why do you care?" she demanded, her voice cracking as she waited for him to discover her childhood terror.

"Just curious. It won't impact how I feel for you, Cassandra."

Nasir continued to watch her carefully, sensing a secret somewhere in that litany of background information.

She turned slightly so that she was looking out the window. Nasir took a moment to admire her profile.

"Is that all? If so, perhaps we should get to work." She stood up and folded her napkin, placing it carefully on the chair. "My bag?" she asked again.

Nasir sighed. "What secret do you not want me to know, Cassandra?" he asked, standing as well and reaching for her hands. "What is in your

44

past that hurts so badly?"

She shrugged, trying to step backwards, but he held her hands firmly. "I just don't like people prying into my life. It's invasive. How would you..." she stopped when one of his dark eyebrows went up. "Okay, stupid question. I suppose everyone pries into your business, don't they?"

He smiled and tucked her hand onto his elbow. "My life is not my own. So yes, I know how you feel about the private details of one's life being fodder for gossip and speculation." The doors to the dining room opened, the two guards obviously aware that he was leaving the room.

"We'll work in my office. Some basic documents have been drawn up already. You will just need to incorporate the specific language."

Cassy nodded as she let him lead her through the amazing house. The hallway was long and gorgeous, revealing a series of rooms that she wanted to examine in more detail, but she didn't want to ask for a tour. She'd been the one to insist on getting to work. She couldn't very well tell him that now she wanted to play. Besides, work was better. A tour might mean too many places or rooms where they might find themselves alone.

His office was a massive room with wood paneling and floor to ceiling shelves on one side filled with books, some of which looked extremely old and valuable.

"Your work bag is here," he lifted the leather tote from one of the chairs where a servant had obviously stashed it. "No one has looked inside," he assured her as she pulled out a pen and her notepad, preparing to take notes.

Cassy shook her head as she stepped away from him. Goodness, he smelled good! As soon as she could no longer feel the heat of his body, she regretted her move. But that was crazy, she told herself as she pulled out the file filled with the prepared transfer documents. She couldn't actually like him touching her! That would be...wrong!

Shaking her head, she clutched the file against her chest. "Is there a place I could work? I'll get these documents reviewed with additional questions to finalize the wording in," she looked at her watch and then eyed the thickness of the file folder, "two hours."

"You can use this office," he told her and pulled out the massive leather chair from behind the enormous desk. "Feel free to use the phone and whatever else you need. I have a meeting with my staff, so you won't be disturbed."

She nodded and watched as he left the office. Did the man always walk as if he were a ferocious beast? He was all grace and muscles, and there was just something about him that was too powerful to be

45

contained. It was like he was a human version of a lion or panther, all graceful lines and sensuous beauty on the outside, but a person instinctively knew that there was dangerous power lurking just underneath the surface, ready to spring at the first sign of weakness.

When the door closed, she breathed a sigh of relief. Looking down at the paper, Cassy told herself to forget about the man and focus on the work. Work had gotten her this far. The males in her past had only brought her down. They weren't worth the hassle.

Three hours later, she'd made notes in the margins of each page and was ready to ask questions so that she could finalize the document.

While searching for the man in question, she was able to peek into some of the rooms that they'd passed by earlier and Cassy was astounded all over again by the wealth evident in this place. It was huge! Who needed this many places to sit?

"Can I help you, ma'am?" a servant asked when Cassy came out of yet another room, this one apparently a music room complete with a grand piano and harp. A harp! Nasir didn't seem like the kind of man to own a harp, much less play one, but maybe he kept it around for someone else to play. Because, of course, every palace needed a spare harp, right? What's a palace without one?

"Yes, I'm trying to find His Highness," Cassy said, taking perverse pleasure in calling the man by his title instead of his name as he'd demanded.

The servant smiled politely. "He has been expecting you, Ms. Flemming. This way," she said, leading Cassy out of the house through one of the back doors. Gone were the sounds of the city that she was used to at her apartment complex. This garden was surrounded by high walls, which were hidden by lush vegetation.

Cassy's apartment complex had a small courtyard in the middle of the four apartment buildings. The courtyard even had a pool. But this area...this was not simply a courtyard. This was an oasis! The pool was beautiful and most likely heated since this was Switzerland. Even in the summer months, the weather was still cool. The pool was surrounded by plush chairs and looked like the perfect place to take an afternoon nap. But all of this was overwhelmed by the man sitting underneath one of the umbrellas. His jeans and sweater still on, he was flipping through some papers, making notes and discussing something with another man who was dressed in a business suit.

As soon as Nasir saw Cassy walking towards him, he closed the file folder and handed it back to the other man who quickly stood up and disappeared. Where he'd gone, Cassy had no idea, and she didn't care. She just wanted to get her work done and leave.

"Have a seat," he said, waving a tanned hand towards one of the chairs surrounding the table. "Have you finished reviewing the documents?"

Cassy laid the legal papers on the table and was about to speak when a cold, fruity drink was placed at her elbow. "Thank you," she said to the servant who bowed in acknowledgement before vanishing. Cassy blinked, looking in the direction that the servant had just gone.

"Where do they go?" she asked, curious and fascinated.

Nasir blinked quizzically at her. "Go? Who?"

Cassy realized that he really had no idea who she was asking about. "The servant. The person who just brought this drink for me?"

Nasir shrugged. "I have no idea."

Cassy was shocked. She pressed her lips together and looked down at the papers. His laughter startled her and she looked up again. "What?"

He tilted his head towards her, still chuckling. "I can tell from your body language that you do not approve of my lack of knowledge regarding my staff."

Cassy couldn't argue with that. She thought it was the height of arrogance to not acknowledge the people who served you. A simple thank you would....

"Woah!" she gasped, grabbing onto the only solid thing, which just happened to be his shoulders. One moment, she was sitting primly in her own chair. The next, she was on his lap. Straddling him, no less! What an undignified...!

"So, you disapprove of my lifestyle, eh?" he asked, a glint of mischief in his dark eyes as he wrapped an arm around her waist.

Cassy tried to look away, but this position, combined with the heat in his eyes, made her want to...she needed to do something. Never in her life had she been so overwhelmed by sexual need.

She shook her head, trying to deny what she needed, to push away but he only pulled her closer and that shift did...something strange! Strange and wonderful and she wanted to do it again! Nothing she did could stop his hands from pulling her more intimately against him. Those hands moved over her body, his strong fingers caressed her bottom, pulling her relentlessly against that part of him that...wow!

Cassy's eyes closed as the heat hit her, pretending that she didn't feel the electric zing when her core pressed intimately against his erection. She wanted to press more firmly against him, but that would be so, so wrong! Biting her lip, she forced her body to remain completely still. Don't move at all, she silently reminded herself, her fingers digging into his shoulders.

"Do it," he coaxed, his voice rough and sexy.

Cassy's eyes opened slightly as she looked at him. "Do what?" she asked, but her body was already moving, her mind no longer in control. Without seeming to realize what she was doing, her hips rolled slightly.

"Cassandra!" he groaned pulling her against his chest. But she didn't pull away. Nothing could have caused her to pull away. Not when it felt so perfect. All sense of right and wrong vanished when he ground his hips against her.

Then he did it again. And again!

"Stop!" she whispered, but her voice wobbled. Completely unconvincing.

And of course, he ignored her, continuing to do exactly what he wanted to do. Exactly what she wanted him to do. What she couldn't ask him to do.

Thankfully, he knew anyway and he continued to press against her, her body climbing higher, closer to that peak. She was no longer aware of anything other than her need for that pressure, that desperate ache that had to be satisfied now that it had been awakened.

Cassy was oblivious to the rest of the world as she rolled her hips against that hardness, that pressure that she needed more than her next breath. In fact, she stopped breathing, her body poised, ready, desperate!

Nasir watched her, shocked that she could be brought this close so quickly. And more turned on than he'd thought possible. She rode him, her body sensuously shifting, pressing and doing exactly what she needed to do. She'd been sitting in that chair, looking so prim and sophisticated. Now she was his. She had transformed from prim and proper, a lawyer and a feminist, into a sexual goddess, intent on her own pleasure. She didn't care or concern herself with his pleasure, which only made her movements more erotic, more painfully, beautifully sensual.

Those sounds! Damn, he felt as if he could climax just from her movements and the sounds she was making. Everything about her had transformed, even her voice. The noises were gasping, desperate, and hot! Every time she moved, every time she hit that spot right on, she made a gasping noise in her throat.

Obviously, she wasn't experienced at this so he guided her, showed her how to move. Once she'd found her rhythm, he slipped his hands underneath her sweater and pushed aside the damnable sports bra, releasing her glorious breasts. The weight of them spilled out into his hands and he quickly found her nipple, pinching the sensitive peak. That was all it took!

He watched in amazement as her head fell backwards and her body rocked as she convulsed with pleasure. Just like that! Damn, she was gorgeous! He couldn't wait to see her like this, completely naked and at his mercy with his erection buried inside of her, her breasts revealed to his gaze and her body shuddering with her release.

Slowly, ever so slowly, her body came down from her climactic high. He watched with fascination as her beautiful, dark eyes opened. Slowly, Cassandra looked around, realizing what had just happened.

He knew the instant that she changed back to the prim, proper lady. His hands were back on her bottom, keeping her in place.

"Look at me, Cassandra," he commanded harshly. His body was still rock hard, ready to explode but he held back, not wanting to frighten her. Five minutes, he thought wistfully. Just five minutes and he could have her naked, her eyes back to that soft, pleading look and he could be buried inside of her, feeling her inner muscles tighten and convulse.

"That was beautiful," he murmured huskily. He was thoroughly enjoying the feel of her round bottom against his palms.

He saw the change in her eyes first, then her body stiffened.

"Don't!" he snapped, knowing exactly where her thoughts were going. "You are beautiful when you're enjoying yourself, Cassandra. And since we will be enjoying each other a great deal over the next few days, I can't allow you to think of our activities together as wrong."

She almost laughed at his arrogance. "You're not going to allow it, huh?" she echoed scathingly. She pushed his hands away and slid off his lap. She stood up, and realized her breasts were still free. She huffed a bit and rolled her eyes as she turned away, fixing the issue by stuffing everything back where it was supposed to be.

When she was once again appropriately tucked away, she turned back around, fully prepared to give him a piece of her mind. But he wasn't still sitting in the chair like a good boy. And Cassy suspected that he would never be a good boy, never had been a good boy and would rarely, if ever, do what she expected of him.

Before she could lambast him for...what? For giving her the most intense pleasure she'd ever experienced and hadn't even known was possible? Or for...? Proving her wrong about sex? Was what they'd done just a moment ago even considered sex? They still had their clothes on!

Confusion swamped her and, swirling through that mass of confusion was a deep fear. Would he mock her? Would he tease her for being 'an easy lay'? Would he...?

Cassy didn't have a chance to worry about what he might think because he pulled her into his arms, his mouth covering hers in a kiss that stole her breath away. Within moments, his tongue had invaded her

49

mouth, sending shock waves throughout her body.

When he finally lifted his head, she was trembling with lust. What was it about him that could send her into a swoon so easily? It was ridiculous!

She needed to be stronger but then his hand slipped under her sweater and she gasped, unintentionally pressing her breasts against his chest in an effort to avoid the intense heat of his hand. Thankfully, he didn't move up to her breasts. His hand stayed on her back, burning the skin and causing her trembling to increase.

With the last dregs of her sanity, she looked up into his eyes. "What are you doing?"

He moved again, shifting his body against hers. She gasped when his hard thigh pressed between her legs. The movement was so sudden, she wasn't prepared for it, so her only recourse was to hold onto him even more tightly.

"I'm just touching you, Cassandra. Get used to it. We will be doing that a great deal."

She shook her head, but he slid one hand sensuously higher on her back while the other moved lower, cupping her bottom.

"Do you deny that you just climaxed in my arms?"

His words doused her with a cold dose of humiliation. "Don't say things like that!"

Misunderstanding Cassy's outraged reaction, Nasir laughed, delighted with her blush. He wanted to carry her off to his bedroom to make love to her. But he also suspected that this woman would consider a sexual affair a violation of her personal work ethics. Better to get business out of the way, so that they could move on to more important issues.

Yes, he wanted her, he thought as he stroked her hips and bottom, savoring the feeling of her lush curves, but he wanted all of her. She was exceptionally intelligent, beautiful and, now he knew, amazingly sensuous. The whole package. Perfect, he thought.

"I will back off for now, simply because you have some questions for me, if that contract with red writing on it is any indication." He nodded towards the polished table where the house transference contract lay, temporarily forgotten. "But this is not over. Not even close."

He released her, but held onto her hands to steady her. It took her a moment to regain her balance and, as anticipated, she jerked her hands away, determined to stand on her own.

When she could see straight, Nasir watched as she tucked her hair back behind her ears, trying to find her control, her equilibrium. It was a hard battle, especially since he wouldn't step back to give her space.

He watched her with amusement, trying to understand what was going through her mind. The emotions flashing over her soft, lovely features changed from frantic to nervous to confused and ended with what seemed like anger, but Nasir wasn't sure if that anger was directed towards him or herself.

Before he could translate her expression, she shook them off and straightened her shoulders, smoothing her features into that bland look that he knew was her business-face. He was fascinated!

Cassy inhaled slowly. She couldn't look him in the eye quite yet, still consumed by the lust, desire, and confusion that had overwhelmed her only moments ago. When she failed to rein in her feelings, she suppressed them ruthlessly, just as she'd done so many times in the past. She'd learned over the years to control her feelings, to ignore the desire to cry, which would only give her enemies satisfaction.

In the past, their words had hurt, their belief in who she was had caused wounds that hadn't fully healed. But Cassy had vowed to never let anyone see how deeply she'd been hurt.

This moment was no different. Nasir was just trying to control her, to hurt her the same way those mean, hurtful girls had done so many years ago. To what end, she wasn't sure. And yes, Cassy grasped that her past misery might be influencing her present thinking. But because those wounds were still raw, she couldn't quite suppress the urge to hide away. Lifting her chin, Cassy reminded herself that she was strong. Stronger than anyone realized.

She tightened her jaw and took a deep, cleansing breath. For a long moment, she stood there, her eyes closed as she forced herself to push down the pain and humiliation. She wasn't that person, she told herself. She might have reacted to his touch but...she wasn't that person!

Opening her eyes, she nodded sharply. Glancing at the documents, she buried her pain deep down inside of herself. "I have many questions for you," she replied, acknowledging his point about the red notes scribbled all over the margins of the contract. "If you have the time, I'd like to get some clarification and perhaps add a bit more detail to this contract and then get the information included in the language."

Nasir watched Cassandra fight whatever inner demons lurked just below the surface, surprised that she'd gone from a relaxed, sensuous woman to a hard, tense professional. It might have taken her several moments to accomplish that transformation, but the professional mask was now firmly in place.

In response to her request for clarification, he nodded even as his eyes narrowed. This was more than just anger. There was something dark and tragic lurking behind those beautiful eyes. Something sad that he wanted to understand. He'd ask her about the brief flash of pain in her eyes soon. After their business issues were resolved. He suspected she needed to move away from whatever it was that bothered her.

She wanted to hide her sensuous nature behind a stiff, tough exterior, he realized. She wanted to ignore that softer, more feminine side to herself, the side of her that was more sensually beautiful than anything he'd ever seen.

He'd held her hand in his that first time in her office's conference room and felt her trembling. He'd seen the attraction in those lovely dark eyes. And moments ago, he'd watched as she climaxed in his arms, felt her body shudder and writhe against his. He knew that she wasn't always a prim lawyer who wanted to focus solely on business. She was so much more, although, as he watched her trembling fingers tuck a lock of hair behind her ear, he wondered if she knew that she was also this amazingly erotic, sensuously glorious woman. Yes, she was professional too. But now he suspected that she tried to suppress that other part of her. He suspected that she knew that both parts existed, but she didn't like the other half, the sensuous half.

He swallowed a chuckle, thinking about how erotic it was going to be to teach her to embrace her sensuous nature. She was such a passionate little thing. So hot and yet, so stiff and formal now. The contrast was enticing!

She sat down in the chair, her back so stiff, it didn't touch the cushions. He watched, mesmerized, as she again tucked her long, brown hair behind an ear and looked down at her notes. He knew she was trying to gather her thoughts and he tried to be considerate, to give her the space. Leaning back against his own chair, he wasn't aware of the way his forefinger was rubbing his lower lip or how his body was stretched out, his long legs close to her own. He was completely absorbed in the angle of her head, the delicate shell of her ear and the enticing curve of her neck. He couldn't wait until their business was completed so that he could taste her skin, explore all of the sensitive places on her body. He would bet a good deal of money that he could make her moan just by nibbling on that spot below her ear. Or maybe along the smooth column of her neck.

Yes, he was going to enjoy exploring her body.

But no way would he allow her to climax alone like that again. At least, not the next time. Maybe in the future. Watching her had been thrilling and...!

Then again, probably not. He wanted to be buried deep inside of her.

He wanted to feel her climax, even if it was just his fingers buried in her heat, feeling her inner muscles clench as she orgasmed.

Damn! He shifted and crossed his legs as his body hardened painfully just thinking about the things he wanted to do to her.

She opened her mouth and he pictured her lips wrapped around his erection, those dark eyes staring up at him as she...

"Will the furniture be transferred as well as the house?" she asked, interrupting the fantasy blooming in his mind.

Nasir had to jerk his thoughts away from the image, forcing himself to concentrate on her question.

"Sorry?"

He watched, fascinated, as her neck first turned pink and the blush quickly traveled higher, changing her cheeks to that lovely shade as well. Damn, she was beautiful!

She looked up from the paper, then quickly back down. He thought it was cute that she didn't want to maintain eye contact, but it wasn't going to eliminate the issue.

"The furniture," she prompted, her pen making a tick mark along the edge of the contract. "Will it transfer with the home ownership?"

For the next hour, they discussed the contract and he answered her questions. She continued to impress him with her intelligence, knowledge, and the ability to anticipate possible issues. One would think that offering a gift to someone might be simple, but in this case, because it was a political offering, there were plenty of issues that might come into play. Cassandra the Lawyer understood the subtle nuances. Cassandra the Woman was trying to ignore the other, more subtle undercurrents happening between them.

When he'd answered all of her questions, she nodded. "This is a good start. Let me include this language into the transfer papers and I'll get back to you if there are any other issues to smooth out."

With that, she stood and, with a curt nod, gathered up her papers and walked away. He watched her, admiring the slight sway of her hips, smiling at the stiffness in her shoulders. Now that he knew her a bit better, he understood what she was doing, why she walked that way.

Oh, he didn't know the details, but he grasped that she was a sensuous person who didn't want the world to know that she was a sensuous person. She wanted the world to see only the lawyer, the professional.

Chapter 4

By the time his butler announced that dinner was ready, Nasir tossed his papers down and decided that they'd worked long enough. He knew Cassy wouldn't agree, but she needed a break. She'd been working since before six o'clock London time, but he suspected she didn't realize that because of the time change. Her internal clock was completely off after traveling through so many time zones.

Stepping into his office, he noticed that she was diligently typing on her laptop, while referencing her notes. But the moment he stepped into the office, her concentration shattered. Her fingers froze over the keys and he smiled at her wary expression.

"It is time for a break, my beauty," he came around to the other side of the desk. "Save whatever it is you are working on and let's have dinner."

Cassy was already shaking her head. "No, I really can..."

"You really can take a break," he interrupted her. Instead of waiting for her next argument, he simply took her hand and gently pulled her out of the chair.

Cassy looked down at the computer, then up at Nasir. Her senses instantly came alive with his touch and nearness, but his ability to pull her away from her task made her more determined to focus on her work. Her thoughts jumped to this afternoon's interlude, the incredible beauty of those moments in his arms...but also the humiliation of having done something so...intimate...with a client.

This was not a good idea, she told herself. But he wouldn't let go of her hand. "I have too much to do to take a break. I'll just run out to a deli and grab a sandwich for a meal. I can work through...."

"First of all," he continued pulling her along, "there aren't any delis around here. There might be a sandwich shop along one of the shopping streets in the village, but the village isn't nearby. So you can't just pop over to one. Getting to any sort of restaurant here in the mountains of Switzerland is more of an excursion than you might realize. Besides," he closed the office door, ignoring her longing looks towards her laptop as he led her down the hallway towards the dining room, "while you are here, you are my guest. My housekeeper is an excellent cook and can make anything you'd like. I believe that a casual dinner has already been prepared for us, but if you'd prefer something different, just name it." His dark, heated eyes looked down into hers. "I will ensure that *all* of your desires are satisfied."

Cassy had no idea how to deal with a man this confident, self-assured, and...overtly sexual. He was an anathema to her world. The men she usually dined with were more tentative, less assertive. They would never dare to pull her away from her work.

Then again, she was usually more assertive around the men she dated. She wouldn't answer the phone if a man called while she was working. She admitted, this was a special circumstance. And most likely, she really should take a break. She'd been working for six, almost seven hours straight. Well, except for...!

Cassy shook her head and banished the morning's interlude from her mind. That was just...a fluke. A stupid fluke that she would not repeat.

Besides, she was hungry. And a break would help. "Fine," she sighed as he pulled a chair out for her. "Dinner would be nice. Thank you for asking," she said sarcastically as she seated herself.

She spread a linen napkin over her lap as she watched him walk around to the other side of the table. "I'm almost finished with the transfer documents and I've included the additional clauses that you asked for. What have you been working on today?"

He nodded to the servant standing at attention by the doors. Two other servants stepped through that same door with covered plates, placing one in front of each of them.

"I have been working on a trade deal with one of my neighbors."

She smiled, thinking that was probably fascinating stuff. But from his chagrined expression, perhaps he didn't like the task. "Is it boring?"

He shrugged as he picked up his own fork. "I would rather be in bed with you. But it is important work that needs to be reviewed."

She tensed, stunned into silence for a long moment. When she could breathe again, Cassy shook her head slightly, irritated with him all over again. "You can't just..." she shook her head as her hunger evaporated, leaving frustration. "Your..." She trailed off and fumed silently for a moment before changing the subject. For the rest of the meal, they discussed the trade agreement, the contracts, and various other issues. She was fascinated by the breadth and scope of his knowledge and responsibilities. He had to deal with everything from hospitals and medical crises to border skirmishes and military preparedness. He was absolutely captivating!

When the meal was over, Cassy was about to head back to the office when he stood and took her hand. "Come. You're going to enjoy this."

Cassy tried to avoid him taking her hand, but his reflexes were faster than hers. Before she knew it, he had her hand neatly tucked onto his elbow and was leading her briskly down a hallway. When Nasir moved towards another door, she was only slightly wary. But at the bottom of the stairs, he turned left, then right, then used a key from his pocket to open a cabinet. Inside, there was an arsenal of weapons. She saw everything from pistols to rifles to automatic weapons and other items that she didn't recognize.

"What in the world?" she asked, horrified and, at the same time, fascinated. "Why do you have so many weapons?"

He laughed softly as he selected two pistols, checking the magazines for bullets. He took several boxes of bullets from one of the drawers below. "It isn't what you're thinking."

She stepped back when he turned around, handing her a pair of safety glasses. "I think that you have an illegal stash of arms in your house."

He chuckled. "Not illegal, but yes, a significant number of weapons. My security team keeps all of the weapons cleaned and ready for immediate use in case of an emergency."

He led her down a short hallway and opened another door. That's when Cassy realized that the man didn't just have a weapons cabinet in his house, but also a shooting range. "You practice in here?" she asked, amazed.

"Of course," he replied and handed her a pair of ear protection. "My whole team, including myself, practice often."

She didn't understand that, but then again, she didn't need to. Cassy would only be in this house for another twenty-four hours, maybe less.

She looked at the ear protection in her hands, tilting them from one side to another. "Why did you hand me these?' she asked, suddenly reluctant.

"Because I'm going to teach you how to fire a pistol," he replied as if it was the most obvious answer.

"This way," he urged and led her to one of the shooting aisles. He placed both pistols on a small counter in front of them, with the muzzle pointed towards the target end.

"First, you're going to check the safety," he explained, pointing to the switch at one end of the pistol grip. "Always make sure that your weapon's safety is in place before you pick it up."

Cassy eyed the sinister-looking black gun, her mind running in a thousand different directions. Yes, she'd always wanted to learn to shoot, but...uh...not like this! Not with a man who could probably shoot the whiskers off a dragon!

She didn't have time to wonder if dragons actually had whiskers because he put his hands on her hips and turned her so that she was facing the target. The heat coming through the two layers of their clothing was more than a little disconcerting. Nasir shifted, moving so that her back was practically braced against his chest, his hands still resting on her hips.

"You can touch it," he told her softly, his breath tickling her ear.

Cassy started to turn around, to tell him that this was a bad idea, but his hands on her hips stopped her. "Don't wimp out on me now, Cassandra. Pick up the pistol. Let me see your grip."

She faced the target and took a deep breath.

So she reached out and gingerly picked up the weapon. Actually, she pinched it with her thumb and forefinger, afraid it might...explode or go off or do something horrible if she held it too tightly.

"You need to grip it like you mean it," he told her. She could hear his amusement. She should have anticipated his next move. His arms wrapped around her as he showed her how to grip the gun. His body was literally surrounding her, almost hugging her as he demonstrated. Even his hands were covering hers as he adjusted her grip. "Like this," he whispered, his voice husky.

She tried to hold it firmly in her hands, but his body was pressed against hers from her shoulders all the way down to her calves. Part of her wanted to drop the pistol, turn around and demand that he do the same thing that he'd done earlier. But the smarter half of her brain, the more sensible side, was screaming to just drop the gun and run away, get as far away from him as she could.

He must have understood the conflict going through her mind because he leaned forward, pressing his body more firmly against hers. "That's better," he told her, his lips dangerously close to the sensitive shell of her ear. "The safety is on, so nothing will happen. Try pulling the trigger. Just get a feel for the weapon, understand the weight, the heft."

She shook her head, exasperated. "I can't. Not while you're so close to me."

"Fine," he stepped back. "Now, feel the weight. Hold the gun steady."

She wanted to berate him, to demand an explanation on how to hold the stupid thing steady when he was nearby. But that kind of revelation would give him too much power if he knew how much he affected her.

Then again, the man wasn't an idiot. He had to know how intensely he could make her feel that damnable desire.

Cassy took another deep breath and focused. "Okay, I'm holding it. It's steady. The safety is on and I'm pulling the trigger. Now what?"

He stepped forward and she stopped him. Maintaining a firm grip with one hand, she lifted her other hand. "Stop right there." When one dark eyebrow went up in question, she sighed and carefully placed the gun on the table in front of her. "Look, I'm going to be completely honest with you." He stepped backwards and crossed his arms over his chest. A very nice chest, she thought, before realizing her thoughts were going in the wrong direction again.

Closing her eyes, she focused again. "You're a very attractive man. You know that. I am attracted to you and I can't seem to stop it. When you're close, something odd happens to me and I can't really explain it. But," she paused and took a deep breath before continuing, "I don't want it to keep happening."

He moved closer, ignoring the way she immediately stepped back. "Why are you so frightened of the attraction between us?"

She shook her head, but before she could tell him anything, he pressed a finger against her lips, stopping her argument. "Cassandra, if you don't explain your resistance to me, then we will continue this dance all night. I would like to have you in my bed and I know that we can give each other a great deal of pleasure. But if there is some reason you are opposed to having a relationship with me, then you need to explain it to me."

"You mean, besides the ethical issues with me having sex with my client?"

"I will release you from that role, if that will help."

She shook her head, horrified at that suggestion. "No, please don't do that!" She took a deep breath. "I know that you are an important client to my firm."

"I don't see a problem with this."

She rubbed her forehead, trying to get him to see reason. "Look, you're a *client*. I'm an employee currently working for you. For all intents and purposes, no matter what happens, if I have sex with you or not, I'll never know for certain I'm doing a good job. Sex muddies the waters. It would cause not only me, but also my supervisors, to question a good evaluation from you."

He watched her eyes, accepting that her explanation made sense. But there was more.

"Is that all?"

She sighed again. "No. That's not all."

"There's something personal, isn't there?" He touched her hair, pushing it behind her shoulders. "Something that is bothering you."

Cassy was doubly impressed that he could read her so easily. That spoke volumes for his perception. And she decided to be honest with him, thinking it would help him understand her resistance.

Unable to look him in the eye, she stepped away from him, needing space in order to tell this story. "When I was a teenager," she began, then stopped, shuddering at the wave of memories. Taking another deep breath, she tried again, crossing her arms over her chest, trying to hide her body from him. "Well, I developed early," she explained.

He leaned back against the wall. "You have a lovely figure."

She flushed and looked away. "Yes, well, the boys noticed that too." She stared at the ground. "The girls did as well. And they said... things...that were painful."

There was silence for a long time. "What did they say?" he prompted.

She shrugged and laughed. "Oh, they were creative. Saying things like how much of a slut I was, how my breasts were the leading factor in my good grades. One girl snidely pointed out that having sex with my eighth grade history teacher wouldn't help me in the long run."

Nasir was stunned. He knew kids were cruel, but those comments were outrageous. "You never had sex with your teachers," he stated emphatically.

Cassy laughed and wrapped her arms more tightly around her. "The boys seemed to think that the girls' insinuations were an open invitation for me to have sex with all of them." She paused, crossing her arms over her chest. "One time, I was alone after school and some boys..." she paused and looked down, pressing her lips together as she remembered vividly the terror of that afternoon. "A group of boys trapped me against the lockers." She closed her eyes, fighting the fear. "If it weren't for a teacher coming out of one of the classrooms, I don't know what would have happened."

"They didn't hurt you?"

She shook her head. "No physically. Psychologically, I was terrified. Plus all of the insults and innuendos..." she sighed and shrugged as if trying to dismiss the problem. "It got to be so bad, that my father enrolled me in an all-girls, boarding school. It was his way of protecting me from the boys and their aggressive advances, as well as the horrible comments. But...there was a boys' boarding school that..." she stopped and blinked back tears.

It took her a moment, but eventually, she was able to continue. "My friends and I didn't even attend the first dance of the season. We were on the yearbook team. We were the poor students in the school. The scholarship students." Cassy shook her head, laughing harshly. "We couldn't afford the designer dresses and expensive shoes that the other girls had for the event. So instead of embarrassing ourselves with cast-off outfits, we ignored the dance and worked on the yearbook layout instead."

She sniffed and looked away. "I found out the next day..." she took a deep breath, needing to explain. Cassy needed him to understand. "A group of boys made a bet. They each had a month to have sex with me. If they didn't 'score', the boy would be on bathroom duty for the next month." After all these years, the humiliation was still an open wound.

"I had friends at the boarding school who believed me when I claimed not to have had sex with any of them. But the boys were insistent and the other girls believed them, one in particular who was a vicious, elitist brat. It didn't matter that I hadn't even gone to the dance during which one boy claimed to have had sex with me. Or that my friends had been with me all night, eating pizza and working on the yearbook layout. The boys all claimed to have had sex with the 'big busted girl'. Apparently, they didn't even bother to find out my name."

Nasir listened, disgusted and furious. "You didn't."

She shook her head, relieved and somewhat mollified by his fervent insistence. "No. I didn't." She turned away and shivered. "I focused on studying. I have two amazing friends and we got through those years together."

He pushed away from the wall. "And this is why you think we shouldn't have any sort of physical relationship?" He understood now and it made perfect sense. She'd been humiliated because of her pronounced figure so she'd decided to ignore any sort of physical connection.

"Yes. I would rather just focus on work issues." Her eyes moved over his broad, muscular shoulders and chest, ignoring the way her heart stuttered slightly at the sight. "Thank you for understanding."

Cassy started to move away, intending to go upstairs, finish the contract, and then get on a plane so that she could go home and forget that this day had ever happened.

"I understand." He took her hand and led her out of the shooting range. There was a guard just outside of the room and Nasir called out an order to the man who immediately nodded, moving in to put the weapons and ammunition back in the locked case. Nasir pulled her along behind him up the first flight of stairs, then over to the elaborate stairs she'd descended so many hours ago. She suspected there were bedrooms up those stairs and she pulled away.

"Your Highness..." she began.

His foot was on the first stair as he paused and looked down at her. "No Cassandra. This is important. Come with me."

She shook her head and tried to pull her hand away, but he didn't release her hand. In fact, he didn't even bring her back into the bedroom she'd woken up in this morning. Oh no, this room was much larger, much more elaborate. And the colors were darker. No lemony yellow color scheme or filmy curtains. The colors here were red and black with splashes of cream.

"Please, don't do this!" she begged, although he didn't drag her to the bed as she'd thought he would. If he had, she would have fought him with everything in her. But instead, he pulled her over to the full-length mirror. Standing behind her, he held her in front of him, his head watching her over her shoulder.

"Look at yourself, Cassandra."

She glared at him through the mirror, refusing to look at her own reflection. "I don't need to look at myself, Your Highness. I know what I look like."

"I don't think you do. I think you've created a monster in your head. A monster developed from too many years of negative thinking." His hands shifted and he held her so that she had to face the mirror. "You're beautiful, Cassandra. You don't even realize how lovely you are because you have this image in your mind, an image that someone else put there."

"Let me go!" she demanded as firmly as she could despite the tears forming in her eyes.

"Look, Cassandra," he insisted, softly this time, holding her firmly. "You're beautiful. You must own the image. Don't let them win. Their taunts hurt when you were in school, but you're not in school anymore. Don't let them own you now."

His words startled her. "They don't own me. They didn't..."

"They are winning. You are still letting their words haunt you. So, look at the beautiful woman in the mirror and create your own image. Take your power back!"

She still looked away so he sighed, the breath teasing the wisps of hair along her neck. "Fine. I'll tell you what I see when I look at you." His hands smoothed down her arms, taking her fingers and then lifting her arms out to the sides, like she was flying. "I see a woman who is incredibly intelligent. Despite a painful life, she's still soft and caring." He kissed the top of her head and Cassy felt the caress all the way down to her toes. "I see a woman who wears a hideous bra in order to hide her beautiful breasts." He ignored the strangled sound she made and tightened his grasp on her wrists, knowing she wanted to wrap her arms around herself and hide her breasts from his view. "No, Cassandra. You're not going to hide from me. Not anymore. You're beautiful. You're not promiscuous." His nose nuzzled the hair away from her neck, then his lips moved against that skin. "In fact, I doubt you've had many lovers at all, have you?"

She didn't respond, her whole body tense as if she could somehow keep herself from feeling the intense surge of need as his lips teased her neck, her ear, her shoulder. "Please, Your Highness, I can't–"

"Call me Nasir." He kissed her neck again, smiling slightly when she shivered. He didn't think she was aware of it, but she was even now leaning back against his chest. He loved the way she was innately sensuous, unconsciously seeking out his touch. Now he just needed to get her to accept that aspect of her body and mind. It would be an enticing challenge, he thought.

She shook her head. "This is a pointless conversation."

"It is a very relevant conversation, Cassandra, since I'm going to make love to you. But I want to make love to the woman you are and not the myth in your head. And I don't want you regretting your decision afterward."

Part of her melted at his words, desperately wanting them to be real. The other part of her cringed, hating to hear them. She couldn't make love with him! She needed to prove herself, to be strong and not give in to the cravings that were clawing at her from the inside.

She would be strong! She could! It just took determination and resolve! "You can't..."

She stopped when his lips brushed her neck. The words simply wouldn't come out.

"Cassandra, you have no idea how beautiful you are, do you?" He nibbled her earlobe. "And I bet you've never experienced bliss in another man's arms, have you?" He didn't wait for her to answer. "Of course you haven't. You wouldn't let yourself." He let his hands slide underneath her sweater, lifting it slightly so that her stomach showed. "Look at your stomach. Your skin is so pale and delicate." He waited until her eyes opened. As he looked at her through the mirror, his tanned fingers explored the pale skin he'd just revealed. "See the contrast? Your pale skin against my darker hand?" His fingers spread out, spanning her stomach from one side to the other. "Your slight size against my larger body." His fingers curled and skimmed along her muscles. His lips curled slightly as he absorbed her reaction. "Even now, you can't hide from what you want, can you?"

She took in a deep, shuddering breath, but shook her head and shifted, intending to pull his arm away. But as soon as her fingers touched his skin, there was more contrast. Her fingers against his wrist were so pale and she was transfixed by the difference.

But it was irrelevant. "I..."

"You need to be quiet, Cassandra. You need to let me make love to you. I'll show you," he whispered into her ear. "I'll prove to you that sex can be beautiful and extraordinary. Nothing to be ashamed of."

Oh, his words were magic. It was as if he could read her mind. But that was impossible. And yet, he was saying the words that she so desperately wanted to hear. In the dark night, alone in her bed, she'd craved the touch of a strong man, a man who wasn't afraid of her sexuality, or his own.

"Say my name, Cassy," he commanded, his hand moving higher along her stomach.

She watched, fascinated as his hand moved her sweater out of the way, moving along the muscles of her stomach. Higher. Higher still.

When his fingers curled around the elastic covering her breasts, she gasped. The feeling was hot. Erotic. Almost painfully pleasurable. Then his thumb rubbed against her pebbled nipple and her knees almost gave out. If he hadn't been standing behind her, giving her support, she might have hit the floor.

As it was, she unconsciously grabbed onto his thighs while her head leaned back onto his broad shoulder. She wasn't aware of the way her bottom pressed against his groin. But Nasir was.

Turning her towards him, he kissed her, felt her mouth open as her body pressed against his. The triumph that surged through him with her capitulation was only superseded by his need to possess her, to put a stamp of ownership on her. She was so sensuous as she shifted against him, so intensely passionate, but he didn't want just one time with her. He suspected that he could never get enough of this woman. She was complex and simple, erotic and innocent. He was fascinated by the dichotomy.

He lifted the ruby red sweater over her head, tossing it carelessly onto the floor behind him. When he looked down, he was almost amused by the sport bra hiding her magnificent breasts. There was only one problem. He had never taken such a piece of clothing off a woman before. He wasn't sure how to accomplish it. The thing didn't seem to have any hooks.

So he did what any man under similar circumstances would do. He pulled a knife out of his boot and sliced the thing to shreds. The intense satisfaction that hit him as the pieces fell off her gorgeous body was powerful!

"Never again," he muttered as he closed the knife and tucked it back in the sheath in his boot.

Cassy couldn't believe what he'd just done. All of the amazing feelings that he'd created in her dissipated as she realized that her sports bra, the only one she had with her, was destroyed. "What have you done?" she demanded, looking at the floor in horror even as she covered her breasts. Her too large, too embarrassing breasts that no man had ever seen uncovered before.

"I've destroyed a crutch that you will no longer be allowed to use, Cassy," he said and put his hands back on her waist, sliding them along her bare skin.

She looked down at the shredded sports bra, then at his hands. Looking up at him, she shook her head. "Your...Nasir," she corrected when she saw the warning in his eyes, "I can't do this. I thought I could, but..."

"Look at me, Cassy," he commanded, his hands still on her waist even though he wanted to pull her hands away from those glorious breasts and feast his eyes on their bounty. He could tell that she needed reassurance more than he needed to explore her breasts.

When her soft, brown eyes looked up into his, he saw the fear. No, the terror. His chest constricted with her look and he relented. Slightly.

"Cassy, what is it that you suspect I might think about you? That you're weak or easy? That you're a hussy for enjoying some time in my bed?"

"Yes!" she gasped, glancing at the bed, then back to him, but she could only look at his chest.

"Then you're wrong."

Irritated...no, furious, she glared at him. "You can have any woman you want, Nasir. Why are you wasting your time on me?"

"Because I want *you*. Yes, women throw themselves at me often. That doesn't mean they want *me*, Cassy." He pulled her into his arms. "It only means they want the power I hold. They are seduced by my title, not me, the person." His fingers dove into her hair and he kissed her gently on the forehead. "You want me, Cassy. You don't give a damn about my title or my wealth. You would rather that I didn't have any."

She peered up at him and he laughed, seeing the truth in her lovely eyes. "I thought as much," he replied, the amusement evident in his tone. "I want you, Cassy. I want your body and your mind, I want your intelligence and your warm heart that you try so desperately hard to hide from the world so that they will see you as a hard core, tough litigator. But I see the soft, gentle woman underneath the veneer." He felt

64

her shoulders relax ever so slightly. "I want to show you the amazing woman, the sensuous beauty you are underneath all of the temporary accouterments you put on each morning. Like the sports bra. But I have news for you, Cassy," he waited until she looked up at him. "Men can see through all of it. We can see the vulnerable woman underneath the stiff suits and flattened chests. I'm called to that woman, drawn to you in ways you can't even imagine."

She laughed nervously, her anger dissipating slightly. Still, she shook her head. "That woman doesn't exist."

He felt something loosen in his chest with her laughter. It sounded so pretty, so lively and he wanted to hear it again.

"Who are you trying to convince? Me? Or yourself?"

She shrugged.

"Let me make love to you. No one outside of this room will know about what happens behind those doors," he told her. "Not a soul. You can go back to your boardrooms and your law office, knowing that you have a secret, a secret that only you and I know about." He kissed her forehead. "Except there will be a smile in your eyes. You'll know something about yourself, something amazing." He kissed her cheeks. "You'll hold your head up high, Cassy, and know that you've experienced something not many people get to enjoy. You're far more passionate than you are giving yourself permission to be, but that's not going to last."

"I'm not passionate."

He laughed as he softly kissed her lips. "Prove it," he challenged as he pulled her against him.

Automatically, she reached to balance herself, releasing her breasts, and she was shocked at how wonderful it felt to have them pressed against his hard chest. The feeling of her breasts against him, free from the constraints of an unforgiving sports bra, was incredible!

When he pulled his mouth away, she whimpered. "More," she begged even as she unconsciously rubbed her nipples against his rough sweater. Closing her eyes, she did it again and again.

Nasir knew exactly what she was doing and pulled his sweater off. Dumping it on top of hers on the floor. When it was gone, he pulled her right back into her arms, encouraging her to continue.

She was like a kitten, leaning in for more affection, more petting. Nasir was more than willing to give it to her. Damn, she was incredible!

He carried her over to the bed and laid her down. He didn't waste time. His fingers moved to the snap on her jeans and tugged them off. He did the same with his own clothes, and climbed onto the bed next to her. Automatically, she reached for him, but he could feel her nervous trembling.

"Don't be afraid, Cassandra," he soothed as his hands moved along her body. He was lying next to her, but when he noticed her fingers forming small fists, he shifted so that he was on top of her. Both other times, she'd relaxed when she could feel him.

Cassy gasped when she felt his body press against hers. But as the warmth, the heat, seeped into her body, she relaxed into him, needing more, needing all of him.

Nasir knew what she needed because he needed it too. So when her hands moved up to his shoulders again, his knee pressed between her own. When she shifted, giving way, he pressed closer, pulling her against him and showing her how to move, how to get the most sensation.

Lowering his head, he kissed her, thrusting his tongue into her mouth until she started to reciprocate. For long moments, he only kissed her, enjoying the way her body shifted against his. When her arms wrapped around his neck, he moved his mouth to her neck, seeking out the places that caused her to moan, to move against him. Exploring her neck, her ears, and her shoulders, he found several spots that caused her to gasp, to whimper and try to pull away from him.

But he didn't allow that. In fact, when he found those places, he gave them extra attention before finally moving on. His hands curled around her breasts carefully. Knowing she was self-conscious of their size, their weight, he teased and licked, nibbled at her nipples, showing her that her breasts were a thing of beauty and not something to be ashamed of. "You're so beautiful, Cassy," he groaned when she arched into him, her legs already wrapped around his body.

"Don't stop!" she sighed, her fingers weaving into his hair. "Please don't stop!"

He laughed softly as he moved to the other breast, lavishing it with equal attention. He loved it when she moaned as he teased those sensitive peaks, and he could smell her arousal, his body throbbing to taste her.

As he moved down her body, her back arching when he accidentally tickled a spot on her stomach, he savored each moment, enjoying her immensely. He'd never been with a woman who was so erotically sensitive. Just about everywhere he kissed her, touched her, she gasped or whimpered. The sounds were amazingly erotic and he wanted more of them.

Maybe if he...his hand moved lower, one finger sliding into her heat. She gasped and damn, if her legs didn't widen, silently begging for

66

more. He knew she would be like this, he thought with amazement. He knew she would be sensuous and adventurous despite her initial reservations. She was so beautiful, he couldn't believe what a treasure she was.

When his tongue touched her heat, he almost laughed at the way her body jack-knifed up. She started to shake her head, but he stopped her with a kiss. He didn't care if she tasted her juices on his mouth. She was delicious and he wasn't going to stop. "Enjoy this, Cassy," he commanded.

Cassy watched as he lowered his head, she couldn't believe how hot it looked to see him doing...that! Then he pushed one finger inside of her and she gasped, her body burning with desperate need. Something inside of her...needed...craved...she wasn't sure what to do. So instead of trying to figure it out, she flopped back onto the mattress, her hands moving to his hair as if she could somehow direct his movements.

When he shifted his hands around, moving those long fingers in and out of her body, she just about screamed. "Nasir, I can't..." she started to say, her head shaking back and forth against the bed, but he moved his mouth, his tongue teasing that nub and she gasped again, pulling back as she tried to get away.

Nasir only laughed and pulled her right back to him. "Not that way, Cassy," he explained. He adjusted their positions so that he was more in control. This time, he didn't give her any warning. His mouth moved and shifted, sucking that bundle of nerves until she screamed her release.

Only then, when her body's throbbing slowed slightly, did he relent and move over her. The look of bliss was possibly the most beautiful expression he'd ever seen. He'd been with a lot of women over the years, but for some reason, seeing that look in Cassy's eyes was more powerful, more incredible, than any of the others.

Sliding into her heat, he groaned at how tight she was, how perfectly she fit him. Her body gave way, her inner muscles contracting around him, tightening, clenching his erection. When she stiffened, he knew that he was hurting her. "Relax, love," he coaxed, stroking her hair as he pulled out slightly. "Just relax and enjoy this."

She laughed, a strained sound that he knew was filled with nervous tension and sensuous excitement. "I don't think I can relax," she admitted, her nails digging into his shoulders.

"Cassy!" he growled, shaking his head to regain control. But it was difficult. She was just so tight and so gorgeous. Her body was such a delight, even now as she was shifting against him, her body trying to adjust to his invasion, but her adjustments were only making it harder for him to hold back.

"Just stay still, love," he told her as he lifted her hips, moving at a better angle to go deeper. Obviously, that angle was better for her too because she gasped and arched, pulling him deeper into her heat.

He'd been watching her face and froze when he saw her flinch. But when those gorgeous eyes opened, he knew that she wasn't just okay, she was amazing.

"Oh Cassandra," he started moving, thrusting into her heat. In and out, he tried to be gentle, but the way she moved, her lips falling open as her head pressed against the bed, it was hard. Hard to slow down when her hips kept enticing him faster. Hard to ease up when her nails dug into his shoulders. And it was damn hard to maintain his control when she looked like a goddess, her hair spread out around her and her body straining towards another climax.

So when he knew his control was slipping, he reached down between their bodies and helped her over the edge. And that small touch was all it took for Cassy to splinter apart into a thousand pieces as her orgasm carried them over the edge into bliss.

When the throbbing finally subsided, he pulled her into his arms, holding her gently as he rolled over to her side, bringing her with him as he stared up at the ceiling. Never before had sex felt so incredibly powerful.

"Are you okay?" she asked, her hand resting on his chest.

Nasir laughed softly. "I think that's my line," he murmured as his fingers trailed along her waist.

She laughed and it was such a sweet, feminine sound, so unlike her, that he was charmed. "I wasn't sure what you were thinking there."

He shook his head. "I wasn't." He tweaked her nipple to make her squirm. "I was only trying to get you to the finish line." He lowered his head and kissed that peak. "Next time, we'll take more time. Enjoy the journey a bit more."

Cassy's eyes widened even as her body responded. "Next time?"

He threw back his head and laughed. "Were you planning to just use me and throw me away?"

Her laughter was instantaneous. "I wasn't planning anything. Especially not this," she said, referring to their naked state.

Nasir stood up, then bent down to lift her into his arms. "You need to soak in a hot bath. It will help ease the soreness before our next adventure."

Cassy threw her arms around his neck, feeling shy all of a sudden. "I don't...a bath isn't necessary."

He chuckled. "It is not only necessary but..." he froze halfway to the bathtub, a stunned expression in his eyes. "Cassy, I..." he shook his head.

Her arms tightened around him and his expression scared her. "What's wrong? Did you forget a meeting?"

He didn't move for a long time, just blinked at her. "Not a meeting." He set her down on the edge of the enormous, marble bathtub. His hands moved to her knees, resting there for a long moment. Cassy's stomach muscles tightened as she stared at him.

"Please, tell me what I did wrong," she begged, the old fears coming back to life in an instant.

Nasir shook his head. "No, love. *I* messed up." He slapped a hand on his forehead, furious with himself. "I'm so sorry, honey."

"Nasir, talk to me. What's wrong?"

"I didn't use protection."

Cassy stared at him, not sure what he was saying. Protection? Protection from what?

"Oh!"

Nasir saw the realization hit her and they sat silently for a long moment. Cassy bowed her head as she counted back through the month. When she looked back up at him, she breathed a sigh of relief. "I don't think it will be an issue. It should be a safe time for me."

He peered at her, trying to see the truth in her eyes. "Are you sure?"

Was she sure? No. The timing was 'right' to avoid a pregnancy, but nothing was one hundred percent safe. "I should be starting my period any day now," she assured him. That was the truth, but she also knew that her periods weren't completely regular. She'd just have to cross her fingers.

He lifted her hand and kissed the palm. "I'm so sorry, Cassandra. I've never, ever, forgotten protection before. I just..." he shook his head, berating himself for putting her in danger like this. "I can only tell you that you took my breath away."

She curled her fingers along his cheek, amazed that he would say something so sweet. She didn't believe him, but it was still nice to hear. "How about if I take a quick shower and get back to work?" she suggested, wanting to retreat to safety now. She needed to think, to process what had just happened.

He threw back his head and laughed. "Oh no, my beauty," he said and stood up once again. "I believe a promise was made." He turned on the water for the enormous tub behind her. Immediately, steam started to rise. "I always fulfill my promises."

He stood up and kissed her gently. "I'll be right back."

69

Cassy watched with fascination as he walked unselfconsciously out of the bathroom. And yes, her eyes were glued to his firm butt, impressed by the flexing muscles. She'd felt that butt in her hands, but seeing it was a completely different experience.

When he returned, he had several condoms in hand, which he tossed onto the side of the tub.

"Multiple?" she gasped, breathless at the thought.

"Oh yes," he said and lifted her into his arms again.

"I can walk," she told him, but her arms immediately wrapped around his neck.

"I've noticed. And believe me, I like watching you walk," he teased as he lowered her into the water in his arms. "But I also like holding you."

She sighed as the warm water surrounded her, soothed muscles she hadn't realized were sore. But as the warmth seeped into her skin, she knew that she'd done a workout unlike anything she'd ever experienced before.

As the water drifted over her body, she started to become self-conscious once again. It didn't help that Nasir was staring at her breasts. "What are you thinking about?" she asked, starting to scoot over to the other side of the tub.

Nasir pressed a button, which started the jets. He took her hand, not letting her escape. "I'm thinking about all the ways I am going to make love to you tonight." He kissed her shoulder, "And tomorrow morning," he kissed her neck as he pulled her onto his lap, pulling her legs apart so that she was straddling his hips. "And tomorrow after lunch."

She laughed, pulling away slightly. "I have to work. You hired my firm to get a job done."

He slid his hands along her thighs and she savored the feeling of his rough, hair covered body against her. Then her core pressed against his erection and she was shocked by the blatant need that flared in his eyes. "You can work in between. I promise I won't disturb you."

She sighed as his hands teased the sensitive skin on the backs of her knees. "You're disturbing me now," she pointed out, gasping when he lifted her higher, kissing her and causing that part of her to rub against his ridged abdominal muscles. The friction was...delightful!

"Nasir," she whispered a moment before his lips covered hers, ceasing all further discussions about work schedules. Cassy didn't mind in the least. She was a bit too focused on the here and now, and that part of him that was once more alive, ready and, apparently, more than willing to show her more.

When he spun her around, she was surprised by the movement, but not unwilling. "Tell me if you're too sore," he said, but his eyes were moving down her body, stopping at her breasts. "Are you okay?"

Cassy laughed. "You're asking this now?" she asked, feeling his fingers slide up the inside of her thighs and sending tingles of need through her.

He looked into her eyes. "Cassy, if you are too sore, you will tell me," he commanded. His hands stilled and she held her breath.

"I'm not too sore," she said, not sure if she was or wasn't, but it didn't matter. Not at this point, anyway. She needed him. He'd sparked something in her that set her body on fire and he was the only one who could help.

He bent down and kissed her stomach, teasing the flesh there with his teeth. "You're sure?"

She moaned, her head falling backwards and she bit her lip. "I'm sure," she told him, even though she wasn't sure about anything. Nothing at all. Well, except for the fact that what he was doing felt incredibly good.

"So, this doesn't hurt?" he asked, sliding his fingers along her thighs.

"No," she whispered.

"And this?" he asked, his fingers moving even closer to that part of her that needed his touch.

"No," she whispered, her words thick as desire weighed her down.

Nasir watched her body grow taut with anticipation. She looked incredible! Seeing her like this after her resistance earlier was headier than the best wine.

"Do you know how beautiful you look right now?" he asked, his hands skimming from her thighs to her breasts, then back down again, slowing across her softly rounded stomach.

"No." She wasn't really listening to his words. Not when his hands were doing things like that to her body.

Over and over, his hands, mouth, teeth moved across places on her body that she had never known were sensitive. It was like he was finding things about her that had been hidden. And she loved every moment of it. For the first time since her breasts started to develop, she wasn't ashamed of her body. He made her feel proud. He made her feel wanted, beautiful, and desired. It was such a change in mentality that she embraced it. At this particular moment in time, she didn't care if the world outside would agree with her. He liked her body. He knew how to make her body sing. This was all she needed. For now.

"Here," he handed her the condom. "Figure this out."

She looked down at the foil package, then at his face and was thrilled by the possibilities. "Fine," she said, and moved back slightly.

He only pulled her closer. "No, do it from here."

She looked up into his eyes, not sure how or why. But she was too eager, her body on fire now. All she wanted was to feel that magical moment when he was inside of her, moving with that friction like he'd shown her...however long ago it had been. She had no concept of time. Her only anchor was Nasir and the way he was touching her.

She opened the package and stared at the condom for a moment. But it took only seconds to figure it out. She understood immediately why he wouldn't let her pull away. The tension escalated as their bodies shifted against each other while she worked the condom down his erection. When it was finally on, she put her hands on his shoulders, more than ready to take the lead.

He smiled as his hands held her still, her body poised just above his throbbing shaft. "Think you are in charge, huh?" he asked.

She licked her lips, her legs tightening. "Please," she begged, needing him inside her. "Just..."

"Patience," he soothed, bringing her closer to him. "Relax."

She shook her head. "I can't. Just..."

"Relax, Cassy," he ordered again, and with extreme gentleness, he allowed her to sink down onto his shaft. She closed her eyes as he filled her up, stretching her. When she flinched, he held her still, soothing her with his words, his voice. "Very slowly, love," he coached.

"I *can't* go slowly."

His chuckle sent a thrill of excitement through her, just when she realized that the fullness she felt meant that he was fully embedded inside of her. Sighing, she held onto his shoulders, wanting to move, to create that wonderful friction. But his hands held her hips still.

"Ride me," he whispered. "Like this." And he lifted her hips, showing her how to roll her hips so that she received maximum friction.

When that feeling shocked through her, she shook her head. "This is... it isn't..." She pulled back but he only pulled her forward once more.

"Trust me, Cassy. I won't hurt you and I won't let you fall."

Cassy bit her lower lip and nodded even though she didn't really get it. Allowing him to show her, to shift her hips, she tried to understand. But every time she shifted her body the way he showed her, the feelings were too strong, too intense. "Nasir, it isn't..."

"It will. Just trust me, Cassy," he interrupted her again.

Cassy kept on trying and, as soon as she got into the rhythm, she understood. With each downward thrust, she pressed against his body, the friction increasing her body's response. And when she moved upwards, she did it again, but it felt different. Not wrong, just different. Both movements were...amazing! Over and over again, she followed his instructions. Her body wasn't sore after the initial invasion, but

72

throbbing now, desperate for that elusive release.

When he shifted his hips, leaning back slightly, that was all it took to send her over the edge, spiraling into that throbbing, blissful pleasure. She was mindless now, unaware of Nasir pounding into her and finding his own release. It was one of the most glorious moments of her entire life!

In the aftermath, she clung to him, gripping his shoulders as she sucked in air, trying to get her balance back. His strong arms held her steady as they both sank back into the water.

Cassy suspected she was like a wet rag over his chest, but every time she tried to move, he only tightened his arms around her.

So she stayed, the water bubbling around them, his arms around her and her cheek resting against his broad shoulder.

It was heaven.

Chapter 5

Cassy rolled over, her eyes slowing opening. Another beautiful morning, another day in the arms of Nasir! She sighed happily.

Lifting her head out of the pillows, she looked around, eager to feel him against her. In fact, it was odd not to be curled up next to him already. For the past two mornings, she had woken up to him kissing her. And then....

She smiled and looked around, eager to see him again. Oh my, how her life and attitude had changed over the past seventy-two hours!

But when she reached out, her hand only found cold sheets. No warm, muscular man, ready to make love to her again.

She sat up and pushed her hair out of her eyes. It was still early so the sunshine hadn't penetrated the hazy morning fog, but it was light enough to see that she was alone.

There were no sounds outside of the bedroom indicating that the guards were still there. And she couldn't even sense if the other servants were still in the house.

It was strange, after getting used to so many others being around her all the time, to suddenly find herself alone.

Pulling the sheets up higher, she wondered what was going on. Where was Nasir? Why wasn't he here?

And more importantly, if he'd had to leave, why hadn't he woken her up to let her know?

Cassy slipped out of bed, a feeling of dread creeping up on her. Stepping into the shower, she tried to come up with a reasonable excuse as to why Nasir wasn't here with her. But her mind spun in useless circles.

He wouldn't do this to her, she told herself over and over again. But as she dressed, she pulled on her old suit, ignoring the beautiful clothes

74

that he'd purchased for her. She felt better, more in control with her wool suit back on, even though she'd had to wear one of the lacy bras since Nasir had ruined her sports bra that first day. Rejecting all of the lovely clothes and the delicate underthings, she stepped out into the beautifully decorated hallway, no longer seeing the priceless art hanging on the walls or the beautiful furniture that seemed to have been designed and built specifically for this house.

Standing very still, she looked around. Nothing. No movement, no bustling servants preparing for the day.

Pausing, she listened for the sounds of a busy household, of an aide hurrying from one room to the next, trying to get Nasir's attention on one matter or another.

Eerily, there were no guards. No aides. No one rushing around. No one even in the house, it seemed. Her stomach tightened with dread.

Walking down the elaborate staircase, she couldn't believe the silence in the house. It had always been abnormally quiet, but there had been an energy in the air, a sense of urgency because there were so many guards, servants, and aides constantly interrupting Nasir, no matter what he might be doing.

There was no one here!

Correction, the housekeeper was here. When Cassy stepped through the doorway to the kitchen, the kind, older woman smiled at her. "Good morning, Ms. Flemming," she called out as she poured Cassy a cup of coffee. "What would you like for breakfast?" she asked, handing Cassy the delicate cup.

Cassy looked around, not even able to sip the coffee because her stomach wouldn't settle. Something was very wrong. "Um...is Nasir, I mean, His Highness around?" she asked, dreading the answer.

The woman shook her head. "Unfortunately, His Highness needed to leave on urgent business. But he asked that I cook you whatever you'd like before your flight." The woman turned to the counter and picked up an elegant envelope and handed it to Cassy. "He left this note for you. I was ordered to give it to you immediately."

Cassy almost fell into the chair, absently spilling some coffee onto the saucer. Was she dismissed? Was he finished with her? She stared at the note in her hand, not wanting to read it. Not wanting to see the words of dismissal. Even his bold scrawl on the outside of the envelope made her cringe with dread.

Cassy suspected that it would have been much worse if he'd been here to tell her himself. At least, with him gone, she could just head back home by herself, not worry about the pity in his eyes when he had to tell her that he was moving on.

The housekeeper was eyeing her strangely. Cassy needed privacy to read the note from Nasir. She couldn't read it with an audience.

"Thank you for the coffee," Cassy said, pulling herself up and trying to feign dignity and professionalism. She set the cup of coffee carefully onto the countertop as she tried to pretend that her heart wasn't shattering into tiny, battered pieces. With the note still in her hand, she blinked hard, not wanting to cry where she could be seen. Cassy didn't want anyone to know how much she hurt. So she pasted a smile on her face and headed for the hallway. "I'll just see myself out."

The housekeeper shook her head. "The driver is standing by to take you to the airport, Ms. Flemming," she called out.

Cassy only smiled slightly and turned back to the front door. She grabbed her tote bag, not sure what she should be doing at this particular moment. She'd never had a lover before, so she wasn't sure how to take such a blatant and abrupt rejection. An outright dismissal. She stuffed the envelope into her big bag, unable to read the note. It wouldn't help anyway. Nasir wasn't here. He'd left a note for her! A note! Of all the pathetic, horrible...shaking her head, she swung her bag over her shoulder and pulled open the front door.

Walking out, she smiled tightly at the driver who immediately jumped up and came around to open the limousine door. But Cassy wasn't interested in more of Nasir's patronizing generosity. She wouldn't eat anything for breakfast because it would be one more thing that he was trying to give her and she didn't want a ride to the airport. He'd left her.

Walking past the confused driver, she headed down the driveway, intending to catch a cab to the airport and then get on the next flight back to London. After that...well, she wasn't sure what was going to happen next. She could only think about getting home. She needed... she needed Ella and Naya. She needed her friends, people who would understand and wouldn't judge. Cassy knew with absolute certainty that they would drop everything and head over to her tiny apartment with several bottles of wine and an extra-large pizza. If several cartons of chocolate chunk ice cream were included in tonight's binge, all the better.

So she focused on putting one foot in front of the other. Walking. Breathing. That was all she could do at this particular moment.

"Ms. Flemming?" the driver called out uncertainly. "I'm here to drive you to the airport whenever you are ready to leave. The pilot is standing by as well."

Cassy couldn't speak. She didn't care who was standing by. She tried to form the words, but instead, she barely got out a brief smile as she walked down the driveway. Thankfully, it didn't take long before she reached the busy street. There, she lifted her hand and a cab driver screeched to a halt at the curb. Ducking inside, she ignored the strange look of Nasir's driver since he'd followed her down the street. Apparently, no one had ever rejected a ride, she thought. Three days ago, she would have found humor in that. But right now, she couldn't laugh. It was taking all of her energy to keep her head held high.

At the airport, she was able to get a flight that would take off in a couple hours. It took her less than thirty minutes to get through security and find her gate and then she just sat there, staring blankly. She didn't notice the other people hurrying to their gates, didn't see the security personnel or the other airport employees as they went about their business. When her flight was called, she waited in the long line, found her assigned seat and stared at the chair in front of her. She refused to remember the large, leather chairs on the private plane on the way over to London. Or how she could stretch her legs out, the way the seat reclined so that she was basically in a bed while she flew across the Atlantic.

The flight back to London was dramatically different than her flight to Zurich. Economy seats were cramped, didn't recline, and she didn't bother to buy the calorie and salt laden boxed meals that were offered. She didn't even see the strange looks from the flight attendants when she rejected drink offerings. She just stared, her mind and body in too much pain to cope.

Landing at Heathrow Airport, she hailed a cab and gave her address to the driver. Thankfully, it was Friday and she could spend the rest of the weekend in bed. By Monday, she would feel better. Monday, she would report to work and explain the extended time spent on an assignment that should have taken one day. She'd probably have to resign because she'd slept with a client.

But right now, she didn't care. All she wanted right now was to crawl into bed and sleep.

Chapter 6

"Is she dead?" Ella asked.

Naya looked down at her friend, a worried expression on her features. "I hope not. She's the only one that can teach me that move in Zumba class."

Ella laughed, but they were both worried about Cassy who hadn't emerged from her bed all weekend.

"Honey," Ella said, sitting down next to the lump underneath the covers on Cassy's bed. She laid her hand on what she suspected was Cassy's hip. "Sweetie, you gotta tell us what's going on. We're worried."

A very pregnant Naya sat down on the other side of the bed. "Obviously something happened in Switzerland. Can you tell us what?"

Cassy groaned from underneath the sheets. Her friends had arrived on Saturday morning and they weren't going away. She'd told them to leave her alone several times now, but they simply brainstormed various possibilities as to what might be wrong. And since they were both sitting on her bed, she couldn't get away. She was surrounded.

Finally, she couldn't take listening to their silly chatter any longer. With a sigh, Cassy conceded that she should just tell them what had happened. They'd be equally horrified, make some sort of excuse to leave her alone, and then she'd deal with her misery all by herself.

Flinging back the covers, she refused to look at either of her soon-to-be-disgusted-best-friends and kept her eyes on the ceiling. "I was sent over to Zurich to handle the transference of a piece of property for my law firm's client. He was the one I told you about last week?" When she felt them nod, she continued. "Well, he was..." she couldn't finish that story, blinking back irritating and pointless tears. "Anyway, I fell for him. Hard. And we had sex." She cringed at the words, thinking she was the worst person in the world for having had sex with a client. It was an inviolable rule! Surely her friends would understand how badly she'd messed up and would leave her alone.

She scooted to the end of the bed since her friends were blocking the sides.

Ella and Naya shared a shocked look, then turned to Cassy. "You had sex with him?"

Cassy grimaced, she couldn't look at them. Her shoulders slumped. All she wanted was to bury herself under the covers. "Yes. I had sex with him. For the first time in my life, I broke down and had sex and it was…" she took a deep breath, unable to stop the tears from seeping out from her eyes. "It was amazing. He was sweet and kind and an incredibly generous lover."

"So what happened?" demanded Naya, shifting awkwardly with her protruding belly.

Cassy leaned against her dresser as the pain and humiliation hit her once again. "It was wonderful. And then he was finished with me. He went back to his country and I'm here. End of story."

Another look flashed between her friends and Cassy could feel their sympathy. "I'm going to take a shower, and then I'm going to order a giant pizza. Maybe two. If you ladies would like to join me in this binge, then please feel free. I think there is wine in one of the cabinets."

A moment later, she disappeared into her bathroom and turned on the shower. She hadn't showered since the morning she'd been abandoned, but it was time to start living again, she told herself. She was being silly. So she'd had sex! It wasn't a crime. And she might have bent the ethical lines a bit, but she hadn't broken any laws.

Of course, she hadn't resisted all that hard, had she? Nope, only a few hours with the man and she'd been begging him to make love to her, glorying in the amazing beauty of his touch. She'd thrilled every time he'd taken her into his arms after that first time. Never had she pushed him away!

Okay, so he'd taken what she'd offered and moved on. Get over it! Move on! She was an adult. That meant that she didn't need to have an emotional connection to a man in order to enjoy a sexual liaison. She was a modern woman who…

Cassy breathed quietly, her pep talk leaving her feeling worse than before. Because she had become emotionally involved! Cassy wasn't sure what she felt for the man but…it hurt. She felt battered and bruised that he'd left her alone with just a goodbye note.

With a sniff, she refused to give in to more tears and self-pity. Time to move on, get on with her day! It was Sunday and she had to report to work bright and early tomorrow. She'd been out of the loop on her cases for too long. She'd relax tonight, watch chick flicks with her friends, get drunk, and then get back on track tomorrow morning. She'd focus on work and not think about Nasir ever again. He was a client of the firm, that's it. She'd never seen him before that initial meeting and she didn't have any reason to think she would see him again in the future. Most likely, he would request a different lawyer for any additional legal advice needed.

So whatever emotions she might have felt for the man, she'd just...get over them and move on!

When she shut off the water, she felt slightly better. She had a plan, she could smell the pizza and she was fairly certain that her friends had already opened the wine. What more could a woman want in life?

Work, friends, pizza, and wine. Just about everything a woman needs!

For the next few hours, Cassy and Ella gulped down the barely acceptable red wine while Naya drank milk. The three of them ate disgusting amounts of pepperoni pizza with extra cheese and sausage. After the pizza, Naya pulled the stash of ice cream out of the freezer, handing a pint to each of them. Armed with a spoon and another glass of wine or milk, the three of them gorged on ice cream and Gilmore Girls episodes, laughing and commenting, criticizing and shaking their heads in disbelief. They'd seen the whole series before, but there was just something comforting about a woman who could drink that much coffee and still form words. It gave Cassy hope.

Around ten o'clock, Naya went home to her handsome husband and Ella headed off to her apartment while Cassy cleaned up before crawling back into bed. In the darkness, she closed her eyes and pretended she wasn't crying over a man who had obviously dismissed her from his life. It wasn't important, she told herself for the thousandth time. Nasir wasn't important.

Her career was important! Getting up early and jump-starting the day was important.

Chapter 7

Monday morning.

Was there a more effective form of punishment in the world?

It was five o'clock in the morning and Cassy waved her badge over the key lock, waited for the click and pushed her way through. It was quiet this early in the morning. Dumping all of her files and her laptop onto her desk, she looked around.

Nothing seemed to have changed. Her office was still tiny, still surrounded by glass walls, and she still had stacks of work piled up everywhere.

Why did it still feel like the world had changed over the past several days when all available evidence proved that everything was still the same?

Shaking her head, she sat down at her desk and entered her password to unlock her computer. It took her an hour to answer all of her e-mail and then get down to business. By then, a few other associates had come into work, but the majority of her co-workers didn't arrive until seven o'clock. Cassy knew that she wouldn't have an eight o'clock start time in the mornings until she'd been with the firm for several more years. She had to slog her way through the trenches first.

"In my office!" Mr. Hanover snapped as he stuck his balding head through her doorway around nine o'clock.

Cassy's stomach lurched, but she stood up and followed him down the hallway. Was she about to be fired? She'd slept with a client! Not illegal, but definitely not a good idea. And to have slept with an extremely important client? Yeah, she should have anticipated this.

"So, what the hell happened in Zurich?"

Cassy's shoulders stiffened. How was she supposed to explain? How did one tell her boss that she'd been overwhelmed by the man's touch?

Yes, she could promise that it would never happen again, vow that she would be on her guard going forward, because she never wanted to deal with that kind of pain and humiliation again?

"Outstanding efforts," Mr. Hanover read, picking up a piece of paper from his desk and read it aloud. "Savvy legal advice, in-depth knowledge of international business rules..." he glanced up at Cassy. "He was impressed, whatever you did for him," he explained. "I received this letter last Friday evening when, apparently, you were on your way home from Zurich. I'd thought you'd be there for one day, maybe two. But the guy must have had some complicated transactions going on for you to be there for three whole days." He leaned forward, his eyes changing from stern to curious. "What's he *really* like?" he asked with a conspiratorial tone of voice.

Cassy's mouth fell open. Unfortunately, Mr. Hanover seemed to be waiting for more than just a stupefied look.

"He said that about me?" she asked, stunned. She should be flattered. Or just relieved! But the letter felt like an easy way to ease the man's guilt for the way he'd dumped her without anything other than a note before he'd disappeared.

Mr. Hanover laughed, clapping his hands as if he were about to count a pile of money. "Hell yes! In fact, this letter was sent directly to the head of the firm! I just got wind of this last night. They're singing your praises. So, what's the guy like? We didn't really get a chance to talk with him much during the trade negotiations."

Cassy shook her head, avoiding eye contact because she just couldn't deal with what she'd done. "I'm sorry, Mr. Hanover. I don't really know him," she told him honestly. They might have had some great conversations and laughed, joked around. But she would have sworn that he was just as invested in their short relationship as she'd been. Obviously, she'd misread Nasir. "He's as much a mystery to me as he is to you."

Mr. Hanover looked disappointed, but shrugged it off. "I guess maybe you'll get to know him better if he ever needs more legal advice, eh?" he joked.

Cassy forced a smile, but she secretly prayed that she wouldn't ever have a reason to see him again. She still hadn't read his note, unable to read the inevitable, "It was fun, but now it's over," message. He'd probably used classier words, but she'd bet that was the gist of the message and she just...couldn't handle it.

"The letter is very kind," she replied, clasping her hands in front of her. "He didn't have to do that, but I appreciate him taking the time." Although, he probably just told an aide to send the letter, Cassy thought with a vicious tug at those old wounds.

"Well, whatever, the partners are proud of you. So..." he shrugged, "get back to work. I'm sure there are plenty of issues that you need to deal with."

Cassy stifled the groan, but turned and walked out of his office. Mr. Hanover was right, she had a great deal of work to get done and she wasn't exactly sure how to get it all finished. Walking back to her desk, she took a moment to stare at the stacks of case files. "Well, better get to it," she muttered to herself. Sitting down, she took the file at the top and, head bent, dove into the first of the pending litigations. It was after midnight when she finished writing up the brief and she leaned back in her chair, sighing with relief. Of course, there would be more work tomorrow, she thought with increasing resentment.

"Where was the fun?" she asked herself as she packed up her bag and walked out. She'd driven into the office today, knowing that she'd need to work late. Cassy didn't like riding the subway at night, and her eyes hurt from focusing on her computer screen for so long. As she made her way home, she wondered if this was her life. If she was destined to work nineteen or more hours of every day working on legal issues.

Right at this moment, it didn't feel as if it was the life she'd wanted for herself.

Chapter 8

Over the next month, she pushed herself harder than she ever had. She worked sixteen to eighteen hour days, grabbed all the cases she could manage, and barely ate. She lost weight, but didn't care. As long as she could lose herself in the complexities of her work, that was all she needed.

After a month of self-abuse, Naya and Ella had had enough. Cassy had ignored their texts and phone calls, but her friends weren't the type to let her get away with it. Cassy shouldn't have been surprised when they showed up at her office. "What are you guys doing here?" she asked as they entered her office.

"We're here to kidnap you," Ella announced, taking the pile of files from her arms. "We haven't seen you in a month and we're taking you to lunch."

Cassy watched as the receptionist laughingly accepted the files, storing them under her desk. "Come on," Naya urged as both women linked arms with Cassy to tug her out of the office.

As soon as the sunshine hit her face, she squinted.

Ella laughed, handing Cassy her own sunglasses. "See? You're trying to become a troll and it won't work. You need sunshine. And a beer," Ella joked.

Cassy laughed, grateful for her friends. They were right, she thought as she walked between them. Just stepping out of her office during the daytime hours felt good. Strange, but good. "Okay, fine. Where are we going?" she asked.

"To the park," Naya said, waddling beside Cassy.

The three of them sat in the park and munched on the sandwiches Ella had made. They laughed, talked, and relaxed for over an hour.

"See? You already look better," Ella said, squeezing Cassy's knee.

Naya nodded. "You do look better. More relaxed. But those dark circles really have to go," she teased.

Cassy rubbed her eyes. "Yeah. I've sort of been burning things from both ends lately, haven't I?"

"Yes. You've missed all aerobics classes and the instructor is kicking our butts! We need you back in class so we don't look so bad."

Cassy rolled her eyes. "You need me back in class so that I'll tempt both of you to grab a pizza after class."

Naya shrugged. "That too. Ella is too healthy without your bad influence."

They laughed as they packed up the trash from their lunch. "I'm sorry I've abandoned you guys," she said as they walked back to Cassy's office. "I'll be better. I'll have my gym clothes and be ready to work out tomorrow," she promised them.

"You'd better!" Naya said.

"And pizza afterwards," she teased.

Ella eyed her friend with concern. "Any chance you could get off early tonight and maybe get a good night's sleep?" she asked.

Cassy looked down at her conservative, black pumps. "Probably not."

"Still having trouble sleeping?" Naya asked.

Cassy nodded. "Yeah. But I'll try."

"Good enough," Ella said and hugged Cassy. Naya hugged her as well and they watched Cassy walk into her office building.

Chapter 9

Cassy woke up and rolled over, nauseous all of a sudden. Laying very still, she waited until the queasiness eased a bit before getting out of bed and hitting the shower. The warm water washed the worst of her sleepiness away but it was still difficult to drag herself to the office. It had been like this for more than two weeks and Cassy still couldn't seem to kick this fatigue!

When her cell phone rang, she briefly glanced at the screen, not wanting to deal with work right now. She was too tired and felt horrible. Besides, it was another one of those "out of area" phone numbers. She'd been getting a lot of those lately and it was really driving her crazy.

She pressed the "ignore" button and opened her fridge. Saturday. She hated Saturdays. She should go into the office and get some work done, but....

Shockingly, she was all caught up. She'd actually been ordered to stay home this weekend! Yesterday, Mr. Hanover had told her that he didn't want to see her in the office until Monday morning or hear that she'd been anywhere near the building. He even threatened to shut off her badge so she couldn't access the office.

Jerk!

Opening her fridge, she peered inside. Nothing.

Well, that's not true. There was something in the corner over there but...she wasn't sure what it was. Or rather, what it had been. It was green now. And fuzzy.

Ick!

She had a couple of containers of yogurt, but her stomach roiled at the thought of eating yogurt. Standing up, she peered into the freezer. Uh oh. Nothing in there either.

With a sigh, she accepted that grocery shopping was a top priority today.

After changing into leggings and a giant sweatshirt, she slipped on a pair of sneakers that had definitely seen better days, and headed out of her bedroom. Her bed called to her but she was determined to resist the temptation. She'd been either sleeping or working every moment of the past six weeks.

Cassy grabbed her purse and slung it over her shoulder, determined to get out of her apartment and load up on healthy foods. She really hated grocery shopping, but the state of her fridge told her that she'd reached a crisis point. She would rather clean her toilet than wander through the aisles of the grocery store, but she also liked eating. Eating was pretty necessary and, actually, now that she thought about it, she was starving! A big bag of chocolate might just happen to fall into her basket, she thought. And that idea perked her up so much that it was easier to talk herself into accomplishing the hated chore.

As soon as she walked through the automatic doors of the grocery store, she slipped her headphones on and turned up the music on her cell phone. She might need to get food, but that didn't mean she had to listen to the annoying music that the store played through the overhead speakers.

It took her only twenty minutes to grab some fruit and a few things for salads. She really did need to eat better. Her stomach was probably rebelling against all of the takeout she'd had lately and the lack of quality sleep time.

As she walked back to her apartment building, she thought she saw a tall man with wonderfully broad shoulders striding out and ducking into a black SUV.

Her first thought was that Nasir had come looking for her. But as soon as the thought formed, she banished it. He wasn't looking for her, he hadn't called, and she had to accept that the man was not interested in her! Bowing her head, she took a deep, calming breath.

When she lifted her head, she felt better, more focused. She couldn't let that man interfere any more in her life, even if he was only doing it in her thoughts. Well, he wasn't actually doing anything, she reminded herself as she let herself into her apartment and started unloading groceries. She was torturing herself.

One moment, she was putting ice cream into the freezer, the next moment, she was about to hit the floor. Grabbing the counter, she held on tight, breaking a nail as she waited for the dizziness to dissipate.

"Woah!" she whispered as the haze slowly cleared away. The darkness around her faded as the light fixtures came back into focus and she looked around, not sure what had happened. Her head was still spinning so she kept hold of the countertop, but at least she didn't feel like she was about to pass out onto the floor.

When the dizziness cleared, she looked around, wondering what that was about. Then she didn't have a chance to think at all. Her body was reacting. Sprinting to the garbage can, she threw up. Over and over, her stomach heaved until her tummy was empty. And still her stomach continued to clench and lurch. Cassy had no idea how long she knelt by the garbage can but when it was all over, she felt horrible, shaky, and too weak to stand up.

Okay, huge sign telling her that she needed to take better care of herself. "Got it, God," she muttered to the silent apartment weakly. "No more long work days and no more fast food. I'll be good," she promised.

It took her several minutes to get up because her legs were shaking so badly. But when she stood, she reached into the fridge and grabbed an apple. Munching on the juicy, tart fruit felt better, giving her body immediate nutrients. And besides, eating apples always made her feel righteous, as if she'd done something good for herself. She never felt the same way while eating berries or other fruits. There was just something about apples that felt healthier somehow.

All day Saturday and Sunday, she ate as well as she could. But it didn't seem to matter. By Sunday night, the nausea was still there. And when she got ready for bed that night, taking off her sports bra was painful!

Her phone rang and she ignored it, since it was just the stupid "out of area" number again. She'd gotten four of those phone calls today, but had ignored all of them. When the phone stopped ringing, she slipped into bed and called Ella.

"What's up?" she answered immediately.

"Hey, do you know how to block a phone number on a cell phone? Is there a way?" she asked, knowing that if there was a technical issue, Ella could fix it.

"Of course there is. Go to your settings and...."

Cassy followed Ella's instructions and, a few minutes later, the call was apparently blocked. Hopefully she wouldn't get any more of those calls.

"Great! Thanks for your help. Now tell me about your date last night. What happened?"

Ella groaned. "We went to a hockey game."

"You love hockey. What's wrong with that?"

She laughed. "No, you don't understand. We didn't go see the professionals play hockey. We went to see his four sons play hockey over at that ice rink off of Pickett Road. It was packed and there weren't any seats."

Cassy cringed. "Okay, so he has kids. Probably something he should have mentioned before last night but...was it fun?"

There was a moment of silence and Cassy waited, eager to hear what horrible thing had happened next. Obviously, good dating skills were not in their repertoire. "After the games...yes, plural...because each of the four kids had a hockey game, so we stood and watched four hockey games." There was a moment of silence and Cassy could picture her friend pushing her blond hair out of her eyes and shaking her head. The woman really was more patient than a saint while in the moment, but afterwards, she would mumble cuss words for the next week. "Afterward, we went to the after-game pizza party."

"Oh," Cassy said, shaking her head. "Okay, so..."

"Yeah, so about a hundred pre-teen boys, pumped up on adrenaline, sugar, and caffeine, stuffing pizza in their faces – not always their own, mind you – and screaming back and forth about who shoved the hardest, who could stuff more pizza into his mouth, and, well, you get the picture."

Cassy laughed. She couldn't help it. Ella really did have the worst luck when it came to dating. "I'm sorry," she said.

"I hear your amusement and I'm not impressed with your concern, my friend," she admonished.

"I know. I'm sorry that I'm laughing. Your dates really do make the..." She stopped. Cassy was about to say that Ella's dates made the rest of the male population look better, but then Nasir's face popped into her mind and her heart ached again. "Well, yeah, you have bad dating luck."

Cassy grunted but they moved on, talking about something else. When Cassy hung up a half hour later, she felt better and grabbed a book. It was only seven o'clock. How pathetic was it that she was in bed, trying to read but fighting to keep her eyes open?

The next thing she knew, she rolled over and her alarm was sounding. Looking around, she realized that it was five o'clock in the morning and she had to....

Rush to the bathroom again. Fast!

Just like yesterday morning, she emptied her stomach, heaving the contents into the toilet. It wasn't as bad as yesterday, or at least, it didn't last as long. But when it was all over, she sat back with her back against the tub and she stared at her toes, trying to will herself to move. Nothing happened. She just sat there, her mind trying to function slowly.

Pushing herself up, she showered and got dressed, eager to go into the office. She didn't like taking time off, even if that time off was just a Saturday and Sunday. It revealed how pathetic her life really was because she didn't have any hobbies, couldn't get into reading a simple mystery novel and she was exhausted all the time. It was better to just bury her head in the sand. Or bury her head in work issues. She could handle work. Life? Not so much!

She munched on an apple as she walked into the quiet office. Tossing her apple core into the garbage can, she grabbed a mug and poured herself a cup of coffee, relieved that someone else had arrived before her and had started the coffee making process. Usually, she was the first one in each morning, but she'd been later than normal today because of her nausea.

She had just sat down at her desk when she took her first sip of the coffee.

And almost threw up again! It was horrible!

"Ugh!" she gasped and pushed her coffee cup away. She couldn't drink that swill! Someone obviously didn't know how to make a pot of coffee!

Her phone rang and she grabbed the receiver. At the same time, Cassy glanced longingly at her coffee cup but there was no way she could drink anything that bad. An hour later, she finally took a break and walked into the kitchen to dump her first cup of coffee so she could grab another. But the smell in the kitchen made her stomach start to lurch, so she just poured her coffee down the drain and hurried away. She'd grab a cup at the corner coffee shop. They had better coffee anyway.

Unfortunately, as soon as she stepped into the coffee shop, she rushed out again, leaning against one of the light posts and gasping for breath.

"Are you okay, honey?" a kind voice asked to Cassy's right.

Cassy could only nod, lying but not sure what else to do.

The woman didn't go away. "Maybe you should sit down," she suggested and took Cassy's arm. "Come on," she urged as she led Cassy over to one of the benches set up for the bus stop. "It's always like this in the beginning," she said softly, rubbing Cassy's back as she leaned forward.

Cassy had no idea what the woman meant. She looked to be in her mid-forties with kind, blue eyes and slightly greying hair. "In the beginning?"

"Can't stand the scent of coffee? Throwing up in the mornings? The morning sickness goes away around week fourteen but the coffee?

Nope. I couldn't stand the smell until well after my baby came. And since you're wearing sports bra, I'm guessing your breasts are tender?"

Cassy had never discussed anything so personal as her breasts with a stranger. "I'm sorry, but what are you talking about?" she asked as politely as she could under the circumstances.

The woman only smiled, her gentle gaze making Cassy's stomach clench even harder. "Uh oh. You don't know? You haven't taken a pregnancy test yet?"

Cassy started to shake her head but stopped when the movement caused her stomach to roil again. Pregnant? Impossible! She couldn't be pregnant!

Cassy looked down at her hands, then at the sidewalk. Pregnant? "I'm not pregnant," she asserted firmly.

At least...no, Nasir had used condoms every time during that weekend six...

Cassy's mind stopped. "No!" she gasped. That one time. The first time! That first time when.... Oh no!

The woman nodded sagely as Cassy's already pale features blanched further. "Yes. It happens."

"But..." she shook her head. "We used protection!" she protested, more to herself than to the woman beside her.

The soft laughter that followed her statement was not comforting. Not in the least! "Only abstinence is one hundred percent effective, dear," she said as she continued to rub Cassy's back. She glanced at Cassy's hand. "Is the father still in the picture?"

Cassy looked at her bare ring finger as well, her heart aching at the memories of Nasir. "No. He's gone."

The woman laughed slightly. "Well, it is a different world now. Women have children on their own all the time now."

Not in her law firm, she thought with rising panic. Yes, women could have babies outside of marriage in the rest of the world, but her law firm would frown on that kind of "scandal"!

What would they do if she told them that she was pregnant and unmarried? They dealt with political clients all the time, heads of major businesses, international clients that wouldn't tolerate a lawyer with less than stellar morals.

Of course, the men in her law firm didn't have stellar morals. Nope, they were some of the biggest hound dogs in the city, she suspected. Not that she'd done a thorough evaluation of the promiscuity of the male London population. But...

She was getting off the subject, not wanting to deal with the possibility of an unplanned pregnancy.

Would they fire her? Was she going to lose her job?

No, they couldn't fire her. Not legally. But she worked for the best law firm in the city. They would figure out a way to get rid of her. Or they would hide her away, give her the worst cases and block her from any sort of promotion, make her life miserable until she resigned.

"This isn't happening," she whispered.

The woman chuckled again. "Oh, it is happening, dear. It happens to the best of us. My husband and I got pregnant..." the kind woman went on and on about each of her five pregnancies...five! Cassy couldn't imagine getting pregnant once, let alone five times!

She couldn't be pregnant! It was impossible! They'd used protection! Every time! Except for that one time and, surely God wouldn't be so cruel as to punish her for missing one time. They'd been so careful after that first time. She'd even helped him with that protection and it had become part of their foreplay!

Oh my.

She counted backwards, trying to remember the dates of her flight to Zurich and the last time she'd had her period.

When she did the math in her head, she was stunned. She wasn't just a few days late. She was several weeks late! She was pregnant!

"Oh no!" she sighed and dropped her head into her hands, staring at the filthy cement sidewalk.

Pregnant!

The nausea in the mornings, her tender breasts, the way she'd almost fainted on Saturday, and her constant fatigue. Was fatigue a symptom of being pregnant? She wasn't sure, but it would certainly make sense.

And then it hit her. Pregnant! Gone were all of the negative ramifications. She was pregnant!

She thought back to that weekend. Nasir's roughly handsome features. His sharp eyes and hawk-like nose, the black hair and his tall, muscular body. He was magnificent!

Would her baby inherit those dark features? Or would her child be more like herself? Would they have her brown hair and brown eyes? Would her daughter have her obnoxiously large breasts? Cassy had no idea what Nasir's parents were like. Was his mother beautiful? He had such harsh features, she couldn't imagine what a feminine version of Nasir would look like. But a male version? Oh my!

"Are you okay?" the woman asked, obviously needing to get back to her day.

Cassy nodded her head. Was she really okay? No. Was she going to have to deal with this? Yes.

"I'm fine," she finally said. "Thank you so much for your help."

The woman laughed softly and gave Cassy another pat on her back. "I'm not sure if I helped so much as informed. But good luck!"

A moment later, Cassy was sitting on the bench alone, still trying to come to terms with the possibility that she might be pregnant.

A pregnancy test was her first priority. Standing up slowly, she looked around. The world was still revolving. It hadn't changed dramatically in the past few minutes. But she had. Oh yeah, her whole life might have changed.

Pregnancy test, she reminded herself. She had to be sure before she let herself panic. She hurried across the street to the drug store and surveyed the aisles until she found what she needed. Self-consciously, she purchased the box and then walked back to her office. She stuffed the test into her purse and turned back to her computer. She wasn't ready to deal with that test yet. She'd bought it. She'd take it. Just not right now. This crisis would be dealt with in stages. Slowly.

She focused on work, getting through meetings and contributing to her cases. She made it through most of her day, but when five o'clock came around, she knew that she wasn't going to make it until her usual quitting time around eight or nine o'clock. She forced herself to work at least until six. But by that point, she was about to jump out of her skin. She felt like she was hiding a secret, which in an odd way, she was.

By six that evening, even though most of the other associates were still working, she packed up and left the office, not looking back and keeping her head held high. She had to get out of there, her curiosity and panic were starting to choke her.

Back at her apartment, she slipped the plastic stick out of the box and read the directions. She needed to pee on the stick? That's all? Just pee on the stick.

Peeing on the stick just...it felt too simple!

Walking into her bathroom, she followed the instructions, then set the plastic stick gingerly on the countertop. Watching. Waiting.

Ever so slowly, the stick turned blue with a plus sign.

Breathing became difficult and her fingers shook as she hurriedly texted Naya and Ella, begging them to come over, now!

Twenty minutes later, they were in her living room, one with a box of pizza, Ella with a bottle of wine and Naya with her carton of milk, plus several different flavors of ice cream. "What's wrong?" they asked as they sat down across from Cassy. They could tell that she was upset, but not sure why.

Cassy tried to explain, but the words wouldn't come. So instead, she opened her hands, revealing the plastic stick showing the blue plus sign.

Ella and Naya stared. "Does that mean what I think it means?" Naya asked carefully.

Cassy nodded.

"You're *pregnant*?" Ella asked in awe.

Again, Cassy nodded.

There was silence for a long time. Finally, Naya asked the question all three were thinking. "Are you going to keep the pregnancy?"

Cassy had been sort of thinking about that all day long. In the abstract, she hadn't been able to come up with a solution. No answer made sense. But with the reality, with the knowledge that she truly was pregnant, she knew that she couldn't abort the baby.

"Yes. I'm going to keep the baby."

Slowly, they nodded their heads and Cassy almost laughed. She could see both of them struggling to figure out how to help. "You'll be awesome aunts," she teased.

Naya rolled her eyes, patting her swollen belly while Ella grinned, relieved that Cassy was okay.

"Yeah, we are!" Ella laughed, diving across the coffee table and hugging Cassy fiercely. "You're going to be an awesome mother!"

Naya moved a bit more slowly as she sat next to Cassy wrapping her arms around both of her friends. "We're going to have fun with this! Just think about how big your boobs are going to get when this pregnancy really gets going! We're going to have teasing material for years!"

Cassy groaned at the possibility of her breasts getting even larger. "They are going to be bad," she groaned.

She looked at the pizza box. "Okay, Ella, you drink the wine but I get your pizza," she teased.

They dove into the cheesy pizza and brainstormed the possible issues Cassy would face. "What are your co-workers going to say?" Ella asked.

The pizza stuck in her throat as she contemplated that question. "That's going to be a problem," she mumbled, setting her pizza down.

Ella shook her head. "Why should it be a problem?"

Cassy sighed, rubbing her forehead. "Remember that scandal last summer when that American senator had an affair with his intern?"

"Yeah. So what?"

"He was our client. There have been too many scandals and my firm hates sex scandals."

Naya rolled her eyes. "I'd bet that the managing partners have several skeletons in their closets," she mumbled.

"No doubt," Cassy replied, thinking hard. "But it is still going to be an issue. Maybe I should just find another job?"

Ella shook her head, her feminist stubbornness rising up. "No. You'll have trouble finding a job while pregnant. It isn't right, but that's the world we live in." She paused, tilting her head to the left slightly. A moment later, she sat up a bit straighter and smiled. "You should just pretend to be married."

Cassy paused with pizza halfway to her mouth. The idea was so...perfect...she had to think it through. "Pretend to be married?" she echoed.

Naya leaned forward, nodding her head. "That's actually brilliant," she said, her enthusiasm growing as the three of them blinked at each other, obviously considering the idea carefully. "Yes, an engagement is a wonderful idea." She sipped her milk as she quickly thought through all of the issues. "You'll have to start off with a boyfriend first though. Send yourself flowers... No, better yet, *we'll* send you flowers. That way, no one can track anything back to you." Cassy and Ella nodded eagerly.

Ella took up the story. "And then in a few weeks, you show up with an engagement ring. A few weeks after that, show up Monday morning with a wedding ring. Tell everyone that your new husband didn't want to wait and you guys just took off to Scotland over the weekend for a quick wedding."

Naya shook her head. "No. Not Scotland. Your firm would frown even on that, from what you've told me." She tapped her chin, contemplating the problem. "You should say you got married in Paris. Nowhere close by. And it has to be some place where people can't check too easily."

Naya nodded in agreement. "And what's your new 'husband's' career? It has to be something good. Something that will keep him traveling. Remember that movie with Jennifer Aniston? She faked an engagement and then her boss wanted to meet the guy. It was a mess after that."

Ella agreed, really getting into the spirit now. "No, you don't want any problems with a fake marriage needing a real husband."

"Good point," Cassy said, gobbling down another piece of pizza. "Okay, another issue. I don't have the money for a diamond ring."

"Fake husband, fake wedding, and a fake diamond," Ella announced with an air of authority. "Just get yourself a decent sized cubic zirconia and pass it off as a diamond. Really, how many people can tell the difference between fake and real these days?"

"Get a good fake," Naya agreed, "and you're golden. Not too big though. You don't want people looking too closely."

Ella nodded. "Yep. Just something tasteful and simple. And if it is a bit on the small side, then the others won't think that your new hubbie is worth getting to know."

"Half a carat," Naya decided. "Nothing larger, because Ella is right, they'll want to meet any guy who can afford a bigger ring. Nothing too small though."

"Because they won't respect you for marrying anyone they think is beneath them," Ella sneered and shook her head. "Nothing embellished. Just a simple solitaire."

Cassy nodded her head, taking mental notes while she ate. She couldn't seem to get enough! Of course, she hadn't eaten anything all day. And she'd thrown up her meal yesterday and today, so she wasn't worried about the calories. She should probably be worried about the lack of nutrition, but she'd eat better tomorrow. Now that she knew she was pregnant, she'd have to be more careful.

"Daisies," Ella announced. "Don't send roses. They draw too much attention. But Daisies are pretty, happy, and would send the right message."

"But pink roses after you come back with a diamond ring on your finger."

"With a note that says, 'Thanks for saying yes' and nothing else. Not even a name."

Ella disagreed. "No. You need to name him. No mystery. Your fiancé is a writer like me. He travels, looking for good stories."

"A free-lance writer," Naya argued. "No one associated with Ella's newspaper. And we can come up with different articles that he could write."

"What else?" Cassy asked, taking another slice of pizza.

"Doctor. You need to see a doctor."

"I already have a doctor and she isn't close by my office."

"Good! That means less chance of anyone running into you for your checkups."

"Right. What else?"

The three women looked at each other, then burst out laughing. "This is going to be so much fun!" Ella exclaimed.

Cassy wasn't so sure. She put the slice of pizza down, leaning back and laying her hand on her stomach. "I don't think it has sunk in yet," she admitted.

They smiled, each of them thinking about the future. Ella and Naya high fived each other. "We're going to be aunts!"

Chapter 10

Three weeks later, Cassy beamed as she walked to the front desk. Another bouquet of daisies had been delivered and she almost laughed at how well everyone in the office was taking her romance and engagement. Her ring finger sparkled as she picked up the bouquet. She thanked the receptionist and carried the flowers back to her desk. That was three bouquets in three weeks. That was probably enough. She'd gotten 'engaged' last weekend and she'd secretly found an obstetrician. So far, the pregnancy was progressing well. She was starting to really get excited! In two more weeks, she'd take the weekend off and have her fake wedding, then come back with a wedding ring on her finger. Everything was going perfectly!

Once again, she thanked her lucky stars for having such great friends. She never would have come up with a plan like this on her own. And she would have been terrified to face it alone. Ella and Naya were already shopping for baby clothes and bringing her fruit to make sure she was eating well. They also stopped by for lunch occasionally, to make sure she was eating during the day, which she tended to skip in the past when she got too busy. They were both taking this "aunt" thing to heart.

"Ms. Flemming, I need to see you in conference room six," Darren announced and walked away.

Cassy looked up from her computer, and immediately started shaking. Conference room six? No!

She couldn't go in there. That was the conference room where...she'd met *him*!

When she looked around, noting that the open area outside of her office was buzzing with normal activity. Nothing had changed. Her co-workers were working as if everything was normal.

She was just being paranoid. Nasir wasn't here. He didn't have time to be here! The man had a country to run!

And even if he were here, he wouldn't request her help. The only reason he'd requested her legal advice in Zurich was because she'd refused to meet with him socially in London. He hadn't actually needed legal assistance in Zurich, she suspected. It had probably just been his ploy to get her alone, away from her comfort zone so that he could…

She refused to think about those nights in his arms. She might not be able to stop her dreams from taking her there at night while she slept, but she could definitely stop her mind from wandering down that dangerous path during daylight hours.

"So, you're engaged!" Darren began as soon as she walked into the conference room. "Does that mean you think you can slow down around here?" he demanded.

Cassy's eyes snapped up to his angry ones. He'd been ignoring her for the past few weeks as the flowers had come in, benignly displayed on the corner of her desk. She'd heard him grumbling the other day when she'd come in with the engagement ring on her finger, but he hadn't said anything about it to her face.

Apparently, he couldn't hold back forever and his normal nasty personality was resurfacing.

Squaring her shoulders, she smiled as politely as she could manage under the circumstances. "I'm sorry, but have I missed a deadline lately?" she asked, keeping her tone relaxed and trying to hide the trembling anger in her body. She couldn't lose her job. Not now!

He shook his head. "No, just the opposite. I was just wondering why it took you so long to get up here though," he grumbled and slammed the door shut. "Tell me about your fiancé," he demanded.

"Mike?" she asked, thinking of the name they'd come up with. "What do you want to know?"

Darren shrugged, crossing his arms over his chest. "I don't know. We have a few minutes until the client arrives. I'm just curious as to what kind of a guy managed to get your attention."

Cassy didn't like the direction this conversation was going, but she wasn't going to let Darren intimidate her. She was finished being bullied by this man. As a mother, she couldn't take it any longer. "He's a very nice man," Cassy said carefully. "A journalist. He's in Toronto at the moment."

"Ms. Flemming!" a booming voice echoed behind her.

Cassy jumped and looked behind her, stunned when she saw Nasir enter the room. His eyes were on fire and she'd never felt the kind of anger that passed between them.

After weeks without him, his presence felt like a blow. He was so handsome, so raw and amazing. All she wanted to do was throw herself into his arms. And then punch him for deserting her in such a cruel manner.

She had to remind herself of his callous, humiliating desertion – with just a note! - and ignore the excitement that almost overwhelmed her. This man was not good for her. He was fickle and abrupt and he'd hurt her deeply when he'd left her. Yes, he might be an amazing lover, but what did she know? She didn't have a whole lot to compare him to.

Besides, what was he doing here? And why did he have to look so incredibly good?

She'd forgotten how tall he was, how alluringly attractive. His harsh features were tight at the moment, the skin across his cheekbones taut with his anger. "Leave us," he snapped, still staring at Cassy.

She immediately started for the doorway, wondering why he was here and why Darren had dragged her up here when Nasir wanted to speak privately with him.

"Not you!" he growled, still glaring at her. Without taking his eyes off her, Nasir snapped, "Mr. Bursow, I need a private word with my legal counsel. Now!"

Cassy could feel Darren's eyes on her back, but she couldn't do any-thing to ease the man's jealousy. She was too focused on Nasir right at the moment, not sure why he was here.

And her secret! Oh no! Her pregnancy! He couldn't find out about the baby! That would be a disaster!

As the door closed with a soft click, Cassy forced her eyes to look up into Nasir's. She wasn't sure what to say. How did one greet a past lover? One that had hurt her so badly, she still hadn't recovered seven weeks later?

Professionalism! She pulled herself together and squared her shoul-ders. "You have a legal issue?" she asked, trying to look like she wasn't about to faint from fear. And desire. Despite his callous treatment of her the last time they'd been together, he still had the ability to make her body quake with awareness.

His eyes moved over her figure, lingering on her breasts before mov-ing downwards. When he saw her ring, she could feel his anger increase. In two strides, his hand grabbed her wrist, ignoring her at-tempts to pull away. "You're engaged?"

Cassy gulped. It was one thing to lie to her co-workers. They were mere acquaintances. But lying to Nasir? That was harder.

Fighting past the lump in her throat, she struggled to say the word. She had to, Cassy reminded herself. This man was not good for her.

"Yes."

Nasir stared at her, his fury choking him. For weeks, he'd been search-ing for her. She hadn't responded to the note he'd left, ignored all of his calls, and, even when he managed to find time to actually fly here to London to talk to her, find out why she was ignoring him, she hadn't been home.

Looking at her now, he could see the lie in her gorgeous eyes. Some-thing wasn't right. She was still achingly beautiful. Even though she'd ignored all of his attempts to contact her, he still wanted her.

Never had a woman run from him. Was that why he was so drawn to her?

He didn't want there to be more. He wanted her to simply be a chal-lenge. His interest, his obsession with this woman was merely the hunter in him tracking down his prey.

He snorted as he glanced down at the ridiculous ring on her finger. "Not much of a man if he gives you fake diamonds for your engagement ring," he growled, still clutching her wrist in his hand.

He resisted the need to pull her closer, to feel her soft curves press against him. He could swear her breasts were larger, softer than he'd remembered. Everything about her was softer, he thought. And even more beautiful. Her eyes had a sparkle to them that he didn't remem-ber, but he'd been so entranced by her the last time, he most likely hadn't been thinking properly.

"What's his name?" Nasir demanded, even though every instinct inside him wanted to hunt the man down and crush him.

"Mike."

Even the sound of her soft, lilting voice tightened his body, made him want to strip that hideous suit off and spread her out on the conference room table so that he could explore her incredible curves. She was lush in ways that other women had forgotten. They starved themselves, wanting their bones to poke out, their stomachs to be flat.

Women weren't supposed to be bony! They were supposed to be soft, to be strong yes, but soft and curvaceous. Like Cassy.

For weeks, he'd been calling her, trying to contact her. He'd resisted contacting her through work out of respect for her privacy. But when she'd still refused to take his calls on her cell phone, he'd finally cleared his schedule and flown here to find her.

Only to discover that she'd discarded him and had not only moved on to the next man in her life, but was engaged!

Damn her for betraying him! Didn't she understand how rare their connection was? Or was she so used to men falling at her feet that she needed to move on quickly, to master the next man?

But she'd been a virgin. He'd been her first lover and she'd resisted him initially. She'd fought him.

It didn't make sense.

"Are you going to answer my first question?" he demanded.

"What was it?" she asked, her beautiful, chocolate eyes wide with... fear? Awareness?

Both, he decided. And something else. Something that didn't make sense.

"Why are you marrying a man who gives you fake jewels?"

Her mouth fell open and he thought about kissing her, feeling her lips tremble under his until his kiss reassured her.

Hell, had he made a fool of himself? He'd never acted like that around a woman, but there'd been something about Cassy that...he'd felt comfortable around her. They'd discussed things, topics he never would have talked about with his other lovers.

Hell, he'd never really conversed with his other lovers. The women in his past had been selected for one thing, and one thing only. Sex. Easing the sexual tension. He was a man with a powerful sex drive. No woman had ever been able to soothe that raging beast.

Until he'd met Cassy. Everything about the woman soothed and yet stirred him. Even now, he wanted her. Knowing that she'd given herself to another man, he still wanted her. Yes, he wanted to obliterate that man from her world, claim Cassy and be her man. But if she loved this other man...?

"It isn't fake," she asserted.

There! Something in her eyes! He didn't understand what was going on, but something didn't add up.

And he was going to find out what it was. Cassy wasn't telling him the truth. They'd been together for only three days, but they'd been days where they'd spent all of their time together. He'd gotten to know her well enough to tell when she wasn't being honest. And his instincts were yelling that she was lying through her pretty, white teeth.

"What aren't you telling me?" he asked, moving closer.

Cassy stumbled backwards, but the conference room table was behind her. She couldn't move, couldn't escape. "Don't do this, Nasir," she murmured with a breathless quality to her voice that she hated.

He only smiled, watching her reaction closely. "Don't do what?" he asked, rubbing his thumb over her ring. "Congratulations on your engagement. When is the wedding?"

Cassy swallowed. She hated this! She hated lying! Especially to him!

101

But it was necessary. "It doesn't matter. You got what you wanted and then left me. I was dismissed. So how about if I just say, 'you are dismissed' back to you, and you can go on your merry way?"

She jerked her wrist away and moved back, unconcerned that she'd messed up the leather chairs that had been placed carefully at each place around the table. It was more important that she get away.

"What are you talking about? When did I dismiss you?" he demanded harshly.

Cassy wrapped her arms around herself and turned away, hiding her face. "That last morning. You were gone when I woke up."

His eyes narrowed and he realized that... she was hurt? But, he'd left a note for her! He'd told her that he would meet her in London or she could stay at the house! She was the one who had left. She'd left and ignored his request! Damn her, what game was she playing now?

Slicing his hand through the air, as if that would stop her rejection, he glared at her. "No Cassandra! I had business to attend to. You should understand that. You of all people should have understood."

She turned around to face him, taking a deep breath. "Yes. I understand."

His eyes narrowed and he moved closer, daring her to step away. He suddenly realized that she was trembling. With anger? Or something else? He wasn't sure but he wasn't leaving until he knew what was going on! "Explain *exactly* what you understand," he commanded.

Her chin went up a notch. "You wanted sex from me. You got it. When you grew bored, you moved on. I understand." Her voice cracked, telling him clearly that she truly didn't understand. She didn't understand anything!

He wouldn't deny that he'd wanted sex. Hell, he wanted her even now! He'd wanted this damn woman every day and every night since she'd run away. Why the hell did she think he was here now?

Even his presence here angered him. He felt like she was pulling him in. He was always in control, always the one to end things. Until Cassy. Damn her! "Yes. And it was good. Great! I want to make love to you again. That isn't a crime."

She ignored the way her body reacted to his words. She wasn't going there! No way! "The sex was fine," she finally admitted, turning away and rubbing her forehead. Nasir had to go and she suspected that the only way she could get him out of her life was to be honest with him.

"The sex was more than fine, Cassandra! Don't you dare try to convince me that anything we did together was simply 'fine' because we both know better."

Unfortunately, honesty was hard. Especially with a man as powerful and intriguing as Nasir. She frowned at him, refusing to let him pull her down again. "I know," she finally replied and turned away again, gripping the back of one of the leather chairs. "I didn't like the way you dismissed me."

He saw the hurt in the way she held herself so stiffly. He also noticed the tears glistening in her eyes and his anger abruptly dissipated. This was the soft, gentle woman he remembered from Zurich. Nasir stepped closer, taking her hands and pulling her around so he could see her face. Trying to see in her eyes what she was feeling, to understand what she was telling him. He gentled his tone. "How did I do that, little one?" he asked.

Cassy shook her head, hating the weakness that was seeping into her body with his gentle tone. She couldn't let him do this to her. It had been too hard to get over him the last time. "Don't call me that! I'm not little, I'm not skinny, and your tone implies that I'm your woman. I'm not!"

"You were," he asserted firmly.

She sniffed, shaking her head. "Not anymore."

"Because I left to attend to business?"

She shook her head, jerking her hand away so she could wipe the tears from her cheeks. They only showed her weakness and she needed to be strong, now more than ever. "No, Nasir. Because you left without a word. I woke up and you were gone. I was greeted by your house-keeper asking me what I would like for breakfast and that your driver was waiting to take me to the airport and your pilot was standing by to fly me home."

He shrugged. "Is there a problem with that?"

She looked up at him, stunned and horrified. "You really have no idea how that could make a woman feel, do you?"

He shook his head. "I ensured for your safety and wellbeing. What is wrong with that?" he demanded, his confusion increasing. He'd gone out of his way to make sure that she was treated with respect.

"It was rude and insulting!" she snapped back at him, furious that she had to spell it out. "It made me feel insignificant! You were a selfish jerk who was finished with me, so you had your staff get rid of me."

He shook his head, not sure why she felt that way. "I never said I was finished with you," he growled right back.

She shook her head, furious right back at him. "You didn't need to say the words. Your actions spoke for you and I got the message. Loud and clear!"

"Let me get this straight. You were so angry with the fact that I didn't

103

tell you myself that an issue had come up so you ran off, ignored my letter and phone calls, and forced me to confront you in your place of work." He stepped even closer. "I have so much respect for you, my dear, that I even invented a legal issue so that you wouldn't be embarrassed at work!"

Cassy's mouth fell open. Could he be telling the truth? "You haven't called me! Not once!"

He rolled his eyes. "I called you many times, with no answer. I even had my assistant call here at work to make sure you arrived home safely after rejecting my pilot's assistance."

Those calls! The out of area calls! "Oh no!" she lifted her phone and flipped through the received calls. "Is this your phone number?" she asked, realizing she might have been in the wrong here.

He glanced down. "Yes. That is my number. My personal number, which is why it comes up as 'out of area'. There are security issues that..." he stopped and looked around, registering that they were talking about sensitive issues in her employer's conference room. "Wait. We can't have this conversation here." He pressed a button on his phone. A moment later, the secret door opened. "Come," he put a hand to the small of her back. Cassy went with him simply because she didn't have a choice. The hand to the small of her back propelled her through the secret door regardless of her resistance.

To his aide he said, "Contact her supervisor and come up with some story. Ms. Flemming is coming with me."

Cassy shook her head. "I can't just leave with you!" she gasped, stepping out of his reach before they reached the hallway where she'd be lost. She had no idea where that hallway led to or where it came out. This was all so...crazy!

"We're going to discuss this misunderstanding, Cassandra," he explained firmly. "We can do it here where one of your co-workers might interrupt and ask uncomfortable questions, or we can do it in a more private setting."

Cassy looked into his eyes and knew that he wouldn't accept option C, which was that they go their separate ways. And if she were being completely honest with herself, she wanted to understand what was going on as well. The phone calls and...had that really been Nasir coming out of her building several weeks ago?

He didn't wait for her to answer her this time. Instead, he led her through the secret entrance. They were whisked down in a private elevator to the parking garage. At least, she assumed it was the parking garage. It looked like it, but this area was shut off from the main parking area. Only a limousine and four black SUVs were parked here.

Obviously, this was a private entrance for those clients that needed extra security precautions.

Cassy barely uttered a word when the door to the limousine was closed by his security personnel and the vehicles moved out of the parking garage and into the heavy London traffic.

Within ten minutes, they were in a beautiful hotel suite that was about twenty times the size of her apartment. Maybe even larger.

Looking around at the beautiful views of the city skyline and the expensive furniture, Cassy refused to be impressed. She'd been awed by his Zurich home, but that had been the site of his callous treatment of her that morning. She wasn't going to be impressed, intimidated, or overwhelmed. Not again!

Moving to the middle of the beautifully decorated living room, she turned and glared up at him, ensuring that she stayed several feet away. "Okay, I'm here. What do you want to know?" she demanded, crossing her arms over her stomach and backing away from him.

Nasir glared right back at her but she wasn't taking it tonight. She was still angry, still hurt, and still pregnant!

"Why didn't you allow my pilot to fly you home? Why did you take a commercial flight?"

She shrugged and put the sofa between them, her pride coming to her rescue. "Because of the way you dismissed me. I wasn't a charity case. I got home on my own steam. I don't need you or your money, your ridiculous plane or your staff. I wasn't going to bother you. You didn't need to sic them all on me to make sure I didn't follow you back to your country." She shifted uncomfortably. "I'm not a stalker. I understood that, when you weren't there the following morning, that we were finished."

Nasir rubbed a hand over his face, guilty that she'd translated his actions in such a way. "Cassy, I promise you, that was not the message I wrote in that note," he told her urgently.

Cassy shrugged. She'd been dismissed. That was it. "It doesn't matter now, does it?" she muttered, glaring back up at him, trying desperately hard to hide her feelings for this man. "I think it would be better if we just...moved on."

He stepped closer to her. "It isn't over, Cassy," he told her firmly.

"It is over," she told him, her hand absently straying to her stomach, but she quickly pulled back, startled that she'd made such a mistake.

Should she tell him about the pregnancy? Was it fair to keep him away from his child?

How would she feel if the roles were reversed?

That thought definitely put the issue into perspective! She knew that she would feel horrible. Outraged.

Cassy looked up at him, still unsure.

"What just went through your mind, Cassy?" he asked and she cringed when she noticed the way his eyes had narrowed. Sharpened.

Cassy looked up at him, startled because he was no longer on the other side of the room. He was standing right next to her and she could feel that heat, the pull between their bodies that never seemed to dissipate.

She had to fight it. Gritting her teeth, she backed away. "Nothing."

He hesitated for a long moment, his eyes watching her features. Then he shook his head. "It was definitely something," he countered and shifted around so that she was pinned against the back of the sofa. "Talk to me."

She shook her head, still trying to resist him. She had to be strong! This wasn't going to work! They were from two different worlds and their lives needed to remain that way. "No. We talked that weekend we were together and, in the end, it was pointless."

He reached up, touching her cheek, then trailed his fingers down the overly sensitive skin on her neck and she shivered, remembering how he had used touch to seduce her. Just as he was doing now. "Stop," she gasped, but the words were too soft. She grabbed his hand, pulling his fingers away from her neck.

He smiled slightly. "I don't think I can," he told her and bent lower, his lips nibbling along her neck, right where his fingers had been. "Tell me what you're thinking," he urged. His hand skimmed down her arm and Cassy had to bite the inside of her cheek to stop herself from moaning out loud.

"I'm not thinking," she whispered, then froze at the honest statement. She definitely hadn't meant to say *that* out loud!

"Why is that?" he asked, his lips nibbling a bit more before moving lower to her shoulder. She suddenly realized that her wool jacket was no longer buttoned up. Nor was she wearing it! Oh, he was good!

Cassy spun around, thinking to get out of his arms. "Nasir, I can't do this."

"Why not?" he asked even as his hands slid higher, keeping her within the circle of his arms.

"Because..." she couldn't think. Not when he was doing things like that. And his hands! Good grief! Those hands could....

"Because I'm engaged!" she gasped and tore herself out of his arms. It was such a horrible lie, but Cassy was desperate now. Besides, the way things were going, she would be in his bed in no time flat. Just like the last time.

Stepping back, she was relieved when he allowed her some space. "I can't do this, Nasir! I can't have sex with you again and then deal with the guilt and the humiliation once you decide you're finished with me. Besides, you hurt me when you left me. I felt...something for you. Something that I didn't want to feel but...that just makes this so much harder." She saw the fury in his eyes and shook her head. "I can't! That's not who I am, how I'm made."

The decision to tell him about the baby was the furthest thing from her mind at the moment. This was survival. "Please, don't touch me." She took a deep breath and stepped further back. "I understand that you play by different rules Nasir, but please understand what I'm used to. My parents were married for thirty years. I'm an only child and, in my world, people stay together. They support each other. They are there for each other no matter what. What we shared...it meant something to me. Our time together was special."

"We can be together, Cassy. Just say the word and I'll make it happen."

She shook her head, not wanting a short-term affair. Not with her emotions involved. "That's not good enough for me." She took a deep breath. "I can't do that. Not to myself." She bowed her head again. "This is going to give you more information than I want you to know, but I was devastated when you weren't with me that last morning. I was humiliated and hurt. I felt like a prostitute that you'd hired for those few days." She lifted her hand to stop his argument. "You even paid for my time through my firm. If that's not prostitution, then I don't know what is," she told him. Staring into his eyes now, Cassy didn't even try to hide her tears. "You paid for services rendered."

"That's not the way it was! I paid for your hourly rate so that your firm wouldn't ask any questions about our time together."

She smiled slightly, accepting that, in his world, that was okay. "That's probably just the way you do business."

"Exactly," he said with a dismissive shrug.

She smiled slightly, and bowed her head. "I can't."

"Can't what?"

"Do business that way."

He rubbed a hand over the back of his neck. "Cassy, I'm not sure what you want from me! I know what I want from you, but you keep pulling away from me and I'm confused. I need clarity."

His words startled her and she blinked up at him. "What do you mean?"

He threw up his hands in exasperation. "I want you in my life, Cassandra!"

As she watched him, she realized that he was being completely honest

107

with her. "This is how you conduct all of your affairs with women?"

His hands fisted on his hips as he glared down at her. "No! What we have together is different."

She stepped forward almost against her will. "Nasir, I don't understand what you're asking of me here. You want an affair, but you don't want an affair. You want me to spell things out for you but, I'm just...I don't understand."

He sighed. "I want *all* of you, Cassandra. No holding back."

She laughed, shaking her head. "Nasir, I can't do that. Can we just... talk about this?"

"We have been talking." His hands moved back to her waist and she didn't stop him this time. "I talked to you more than I have ever talked to a woman."

She couldn't stop the amusement when he shook his head. It was almost as if he couldn't believe he'd had conversations with her. "And was it horrible?"

He thought about that question for a moment, then looked startled as he said, "No. I enjoyed our conversations."

Her smile brightened. "And normal people say goodbye when emergencies happen, so the other party's feelings aren't hurt."

His hand lifted, his palm cupping her jaw. "I hurt your feelings," he whispered.

She didn't have to confirm that statement. He could see it in her eyes and it explained why she'd been so angry with him. "I'm sorry. That was not my intention. I didn't know that you would react that way."

Her anger melted away with his words. "I didn't understand why you'd left."

He pulled her closer, pressing his lips to her forehead gently. It wasn't a sexual kiss, but comforting. "I should have known that you were different, that you might not understand the rules."

She pulled away, unaware that her fingers slid over the muscles on his chest. "What are some of the other rules?" she asked, seriously interested.

Amusement and desire lit his eyes. "A woman has to be sensuous," he kissed her neck again, "beautiful," he kissed her ear, nibbling slightly and she laughed, "and mine," he finished and lifted her into his arms.

Cassy knew that something was wrong, but she couldn't think long enough to figure it out. She was blissfully back in Nasir's arms and her heart had melted with his explanation. He hadn't abandoned her. He hadn't dismissed her from his life. It was all just a misunderstanding!

Chapter 11

Cassy woke up and looked around, startled once again to realize that she was not in her bed. Not in her apartment. And worst of all, she was not alone.

"Oh no," she gasped and hurried out of bed, as gently as possible so that she didn't wake Nasir. The morning sickness hit her particularly hard this morning. She'd spoken to her doctor about it on her last pre-natal appointment and she'd learned that keeping food in her stomach was actually the best way to avoid morning sickness. Skipping dinner last night had not been a good idea, but she hadn't been able to think about food while Nasir made love to her over and over again.

She made it to the bathroom just in time. Her baby wasn't patient this morning and she gripped the toilet with both hands as her stomach heaved and protested last night's abuse.

When there was nothing left in her stomach, she leaned back against the marble tiles, her body weak and shaking. Good grief, she hated this! The morning sickness was miserable and she hadn't eaten properly again. She stroked her stomach, thinking about the tiny cells that were forming into her child. She had to do better, she thought.

She slipped her arms into the thick, terrycloth robe that was hanging on the back of the door, tightening the belt around her waist. Soon, she wouldn't have a waistline and that thought was exciting.

But then she caught her image in the beveled mirror and gasped. She looked horrible! Her face was pale, her lips almost white, her hair was a massive tangle, and her eyes seemed too large for her face. Quickly, she grabbed some mouthwash and tried to tidy her appearance. But when she couldn't seem to get her hair in any semblance of order, a shower was the only solution. She felt drained, but she knew that showering was essential. Both for her body's comfort as well as for her state of mind. She couldn't let Nasir see her like this!

The shower helped her feel human again. She stood under the spray for a long time. She'd just picked up the soap when she heard movement and glanced over. Nasir was standing there, watching her. She gasped and pulled backwards, frantically searching for something to cover her nakedness. "Nasir, you can't..."

She stopped talking when he laughed softly and moved closer.

"I can't what?" he asked as he stepped into the glass enclosed shower area. It wasn't a small space. In fact, there was plenty of room, enough to allow three or four other people to shower at the same time, and no one would feel crowded!

She looked lovely, he thought. She was a bit pale, but he put that down to the fact that he'd kept her up late last night. He couldn't help it. Every time he thought about her, every time she'd shifted in her sleep, her naked body woke him up and he had to make love to her all over again. If she'd said no, he would have respected her wishes. He was trying to change, knowing she wasn't like his previous lovers. He didn't completely understand why or all the different ways that she was different, but the truth was there and, until he grasped the nuances of her differences, Nasir wanted to be wary and careful. He remembered his plan to marry Cassandra, how he'd wanted her to be safe, to learn to shoot and protect herself. He'd forgotten that plan over the past several weeks, too angry with her departure to think beyond punishing her for putting him through hell.

Now he wondered what he could do to get her to abandon the ass that had moved into her life.

"You hurried out of bed," he growled into her ear as his hands slid down her back.

Cassy gasped, trying to gather her wits. His hands were everywhere and her body couldn't help but respond. "Nasir, we can't..."

"You keep saying that," he grumbled, cupping her breasts. "And yet, I keep proving that we can."

She couldn't argue, not when his mouth covered her nipple and started to tease the overly sensitive flesh. She grabbed his head, trying to push him away but he wouldn't stop. He simply moved to her other nipple.

"Nasir!" she gasped, her body ready to climax just from that stimulation. She pressed her legs together, fighting back the pleasure. She shouldn't be doing this! Cassy knew she should be getting out of here so that she wasn't hurt again.

"Don't do that," he commanded and spun her around. Cassy's hands slapped against the marble tile of the wall, dizziness hitting her fast. It took her several moments to get her head to stop spinning. By that time, he'd already donned a condom and was moving his hand up and down her spine. She arched into his touch, feeling her body begging for him. Dizziness and nausea were gone. All that mattered was Nasir filling her up so that she could find a bit of relief from this overwhelming desire.

As she felt his erection pressing into her from behind, she was startled at first. It felt incredible! She bent more, taking him into her body, needing more of him. When he slowed his long, wonderful thrusts, Cassy reached behind her, trying to pull him in deeper, but he only laughed and placed her hand back on the wall. "No moving," he commanded with a deep, husky voice. "I want you just like this while I have my way with you."

Cassy whimpered and pressed her hips back, still trying to take him deeper. He gripped her hips, holding her still. Slowly, he filled her up, then pulled back only to press into her heat. "You're incredible, Cassy," he murmured as he thrust himself deeply in and out of her. Reaching around, one hand teased her nipple while the other teased that sensitive bud that needed his attention. She was so turned on, the dual stimulation drove her over the edge faster than she'd thought possible. Her climax went on and on as he pounded into her. She wanted to beg him to stop, but she was already climbing that cliff again so she could only whimper and beg him to continue, to go faster. Harder!

Nasir watched as his body moved in and out of hers. He wanted this to last, to prolong this feeling. She was so tight, so hot and wet for him and it had nothing to do with the shower behind him. It was all her.

When he felt her body climax again, he couldn't hold back his own orgasm. She was too perfect and her inner muscles clenched him tightly, bringing him right along with her.

Afterwards, he stood there, holding her, the water pounding down on them as he felt her body slowly stop trembling. "Are you okay?" he finally asked, afraid he might have been too rough this time.

He pulled out of her body slowly, holding her tenderly. When she turned around, her arms wrapped around his neck, he held her close. He'd never liked when a woman touched him after sex, but Cassy was the exception. He couldn't let her go. When she moved, his arms tightened around her. He wanted to hold her against him, to feel her heartbeat against his own.

Weeks ago, he'd left her warm body and cursed the obligations that had taken him away from the warmth of her body. But he wasn't going to do that again.

"Let me dry you off," he whispered into her ear.

He loosened his hold, but only so that he could lift her into his arms and carry her over to a stool so that he could dry her with a white, fluffy towel. "You're so beautiful," he said as he rubbed the towel over her legs, smoothing the drops of water away. He loved the way she blushed, her soft skin turning pink all the way down to her lovely, full breasts.

"I'm ordinary," she countered, tucking her wet hair behind her ear.

He shook his head. "You are not ordinary in any way, Cassy," he argued, kissing the inside of her thigh. She pulled away, but he smiled. "I know, you're tender from last night as well as this morning. And I'm sorry about that." He looked up at her, the heat still in his eyes but she could tell that it was banked at the moment. Her heart melted just a bit more because of his gentle touch and understanding.

Darn it, she was falling in love with this man! After being an absolute jerk, he'd been sweet and gentle, telling her that she meant something to him. It wasn't...

She stiffened and he looked up at her. It wasn't love on his part, she reminded herself firmly. But was she in love with him?

Impossible! She hadn't known him long enough to be in love with him. One has to know a person, truly know who they are and how they thought, to love someone.

It was just desire, she told herself. Simple lust.

"What time is it?" she asked, trying to distract him from the question in his eyes.

"About seven, I suppose," he replied, moving the towel up her legs.

Seven o'clock? Cassy jumped. "Seven in the morning?"

"Yes. Is that a problem?"

She almost raced out of the room, grabbing the towel in his hands and covering her nakedness with it. "Yes! I need to get to work! I have an important deposition to help with this afternoon and I haven't submitted my portion of the questions." She grabbed her clothes and started pulling them on, frantically trying to figure out how to get back home so she could get fresh clothes and still make it into the office on time. She grabbed her watch, not sure what to do.

"Cassy, slow down. You need to eat breakfast."

She shook her head carefully, refusing to acknowledge the nausea that was threatening again. "I'll grab something from the café in my building when I get there. I still need to run home and change clothes."

"You don't need to do that. I had an assistant get you something to wear."

He walked over to a closet and pulled out a beautiful, sage green suit. Her fingers froze, still gripping the pantyhose, as she stared at the stunning business suit.

It wasn't something she would normally wear, preferring black or navy for her work outfits. But this was a soft green that would be perfect for an ultra-conservative law firm. It wasn't exactly a suit though. It was a sheath dress with a bolero jacket pulling the whole look together.

"Will this suffice?" he asked, a dark eyebrow lifting as he stared down at her with barely suppressed amusement.

She started to shake her head. The suit was obviously expensive and beautifully designed but...it was too expensive! This suit was way out of her budget. "I can't accept that," she said.

He looked at the suit, then at her. "Why not? It would look perfect with your eyes."

He was right and she was shocked that he'd even thought something like that, much less acted on it. "It's lovely. But it's too expensive."

Nasir would have laughed if he hadn't realized she was serious. Taking a different tack, he tried again. "I would feel honored if you would wear this today and think of me," he said softly, watching her face carefully. He knew the exact moment she changed her mind. Her lips slowly curled upwards, her eyes softened, and he felt a sense of victory and anticipation.

"For you," she agreed and stood up. "Thank you," she stood on her toes so she could kiss him. "It really is a beautiful suit."

"You will make it lovely," he argued. He pulled back and glanced at his watch. "What time do you usually arrive at work?" he asked.

Cassy pushed her fingers through her hair, not sure what to do with it. She didn't have her normal styling tools with her. "I try to get into the office at seven," she told him, bracing for him to say that was too early. Even Cassy knew that it was too early. Normal people didn't work eighteen to twenty hour days, she thought. Then something occurred to her.

"Where's my ring?" she asked, looking around.

Nasir reached into his pocket and pulled something out. "That other ring was fake, my dear. This one," he lifted her hand and slid a beautiful diamond ring onto her finger, "is not."

Cassy stared at the ring, stunned by its beauty. For a long moment, she just stared at the ring, her heart pounding. Surely he wasn't...he didn't mean...this ring couldn't represent what she thought it represented!

"I want no misunderstandings when you leave me this time, Cassandra," he continued, his voice firm as his fingers moved over her hand, closing her own fingers over the ring. "I want you to marry me. I don't know who this other man is, but leave him. You can't respond to me the way you do and not feel something for me. Not you."

She stared at him, her dark eyes lifting slowly up to meet his determined gaze. "You...you want to marry me?" she whispered.

"More than I'd ever thought possible," he told her. "And if you'd read that note, you would have read that I wanted to discuss a future with you, Cassandra."

Unfortunately, her stomach growled at that moment and he sighed. "Breakfast. You need food. I, uh, distracted you last night, didn't I?" He smiled smugly. "Why don't you dress and meet me in the dining room? We'll eat breakfast together and, throughout the day, you can think about my proposal."

She dressed quickly in the beautiful suit, amazed at how it changed her figure. Her other suits were thick and bulky, the material stiff so that it didn't cling to any part of her figure. She'd done that intentionally, wanting her work to be taken seriously.

But this suit...it was stunning! It didn't cling to her curves, but it smoothed over them. Her breasts were still flattened by the sports bra she pulled on, but this suit was much more flattering. It enhanced instead of smothered. It warmed her pale skin so it looked creamy.

For a long moment, she stared at her figure in the mirror, her fingers sliding down over her still-flat stomach.

"I didn't know," she whispered to her reflection.

With a sigh of pleasure, she turned away, slipping her feet into the black shoes she'd worn yesterday. They weren't as elegant as the suit, but they'd work well enough.

When she stepped out of the bedroom, Cassy felt...different. A smile curved at the corners of her lips and she searched out Nasir, eager to see his reaction to her figure in this suit.

"You look lovely," he said as soon as he saw her.

"Thank you," she whispered, feeling pretty, but still self-conscious.

He held out a chair at the polished table for her. Whoever was cooking loved cheese, she thought, looking around as her stomach growled slightly.

At that same moment, a servant appeared with a silver pot of steaming coffee and...Cassy shook her head, her hand flying to cover her mouth. "Bathroom!" she gasped.

Nasir stared at her for a stunned moment, but seeing the frantic look in her eyes, he pointed towards a door.

Cassy stared, then hurried forward, racing for the door. But it wasn't a bathroom.

"This way, ma'am," the servant exclaimed, quickly setting the coffee pot aside on a beautifully polished side board and led the way down the hallway. She opened a door and Cassy threw herself at the toilet. She didn't have anything in her stomach so she didn't throw up. But the heaving was painful and humiliating. She wanted to order someone to close the door, to give her some privacy, but her stomach wouldn't give her a moment to ask.

At some point, she felt gentle hands pulling her hair back. At some level, Cassy knew that it was Nasir standing next to her, but she was too miserable to acknowledge him.

Finally, after several minutes of misery, her stomach relaxed enough for her to take a breath. A warm, wet cloth was handed to her and she took it gratefully, wiping her mouth before stumbling to her feet.

Thankfully, Nasir's strong arms held her against him. Cassy thought about pulling away, but she felt too weak to speak at the moment. Thankfully, he didn't seem to need any words. His arms held her close while one hand moved soothingly down her back and Cassy simply absorbed the feeling of being cherished.

"You're pregnant," he said, breaking the silence.

Cassy tensed for a moment, then sighed and relaxed against him. "Yes."

He pulled away, but kept his arms around her. "Is it my child?" he asked.

Cassy nodded, hiding her face in his chest. "There is no other man," she admitted.

"Could you explain the engagement ring you were wearing yester-day?"

Cassy's hand slid from his shoulder to his chest, the real diamond sparkling in the overhead light from the bathroom. "Fake diamond," she finally admitted. "And fake engagement. There is no other man. I discovered I was pregnant several weeks ago and..." she shrugged. "My law firm is very conservative, Nasir. They won't outright fire me for being pregnant and unmarried, but they will slow down my career, and make my life miserable."

He sighed and pulled her in once again so that her cheek was resting against his chest. "This is my fault," he groaned. "I forgot protection that first night."

She smiled, curling closer to him. "I'm an intelligent woman, Nasir. I am fully aware of the consequences of unprotected sex. I was just as responsible."

His hand moved from her back to her hair, tugging gently until she looked up at him. "You were inexperienced that first time, my dear. It was *my* responsibility." He sighed, shaking his head. "I can't pretend to be upset about this though. I'm thrilled." He hugged her again. "We will be married quickly."

Cassy stiffened in his arms. "No, we won't!" she argued, pulling out of his arms. She looked around, almost laughing because they were still standing in the bathroom! "I can't have this discussion right now." Moving towards the doorway, she pulled it open and...stopped as a wave of dizziness hit her. Once again, Nasir's strong arms held her steady until the world stopped spinning.

"Thank you," she whispered, tilting her head slightly. But she didn't turn all the way and look at him. Instead, as soon as the dizziness eased, she continued moving out of the bathroom, but much slower this time.

Nasir measured his steps so that he walked beside her, watching her face. "How are you feeling?" he asked.

Cassy sighed. "Um...well, besides the morning sickness, the dizziness, the abhorrence at the smell of..." she stopped, seeing the servant standing beside the table with that silver coffee pot. "Coffee."

Nasir followed her gaze and realized what was going on. "I'll have coffee later," he told the woman. Immediately, she nodded and left, taking the coffee with her.

He sensed her relief as she slowly stepped closer to the breakfast table. "Thank you," she whispered.

Her lips were pale as she slipped into the chair Nasir held out for her. "You need to eat," he announced firmly, irritated that his woman wasn't feeling well. "And then I'll have a doctor check on you. I want..."

She lifted a hand, stopping his words.

"I've seen a doctor twice already and I'm fine. I need to eat more, but the baby is fine and..." she stopped, her heartwarming at his words. "The baby's heartbeat is strong," she finished in a whisper.

"You've heard our son's heartbeat?" he demanded, a surge of emotion hitting him unlike anything he'd ever experienced before.

Cassy smiled slightly and he watched as her hand stroked her stomach. "It's going to be a girl," she told him.

His eyes watched her hand, unable to pull his gaze away. "You know this already?" he asked.

She laughed. "No. I don't *know.*" She patted her tummy and he looked down again. "I'm not sure that she even knows it yet. I'm only eight weeks pregnant, Nasir. She's only about an inch long."

He sat down in the chair beside Cassy, stunned and...in awe. "A girl!"

116

he murmured, still looking stunned. But he revived quickly. "Cassandra, you will become my wife," he ordered.

She laughed, suddenly feeling wonderful. "No, I won't," she replied softly. "Having a child is not a good enough reason to be married."

"And yet, you were willing to pretend to marry another man simply because you are pregnant."

"That's different, and you know exactly why."

"The issue is the same for me, Cassandra. We must be married before our child is born. You were willing to create an image for your employer of a happily married woman because you know that's what they consider to be right and good. The same is true for my people. They want their future ruler to be born to *my wife*. We must be married, Cassandra." He knew that she was going to reject his proposal and he laid a hand over hers. "If not for me, then do it for our child. This child needs the protection of my name more than you know."

Cassy heard his words and a fear hit her. "Is our baby in danger?" she asked.

He looked at her carefully and she swallowed. "Yes. Not just our child, but you are in danger too, Cassandra. As the mother of my child, my enemies would try to hurt you in order to hurt me. We must get married so that I can protect you with my name and the resources of my country."

And that was that, she thought as her face fell. A marriage of convenience.

"No!" he growled.

Her eyebrows shot up. "No?"

He stood up and started pacing. He looked so ferocious, that the servant carrying two plates froze and turned around, skittering back into the kitchen. Cassy watched, covering her mouth with her hand to hide her amusement.

"No, our relationship will not be like that! We will have a good marriage, Cassandra!" He paced a bit more, the urgency in his expression becoming harder. "You will love me. I will make it so."

Her heart skipped several beats with that statement. "You will?"

"Yes!" He paced some more, rubbing a hand along his neck. "I will...I will become the man you can love. I will do whatever it takes!"

Her heart melted. He'd never shown any vulnerability or weakness around her. And yet, here he was, trying to figure out how to make her fall in love with him.

"Yes, you've already done that. But..."

He stopped, his eyes lighting onto her. "What do you mean? What have I done?"

Cassy pulled back, startled by the heat in his eyes. "Well, you've...I'm in love with you right now, Nasir. But..."

Once again, she stopped speaking when he moved quickly around the table, getting down on one knee as he took her hands in his. "Say it again."

Cassy didn't want to say it again. Not this way. "Nasir, we can't..."

His fingers tightened on hers. "Say the words, Cassandra. I've been through hell over the past several weeks, trying to figure out how to win your heart. Are you telling me that you...love me already?"

She saw the question in his eyes, and the hope. Something she'd never thought she'd ever see! "Yes, I love you, Nasir."

"But...You left me in Zurich! You wouldn't speak to me!"

She sighed, bowing her head. "Nasir, I thought you'd dismissed me in Zurich and I was...hurt. Crushed, actually."

"But...you didn't call me? You didn't tell me anything."

Cassy nodded, feeling his pain in her chest. After the past several hours, hearing his words and the assurance that he hadn't left her in Zurich, she felt a deep guilt over her assumptions. "Yes. I didn't...I didn't read your note. I still haven't. But with my past, with what happened to me all those years ago, I didn't really think, Nasir. I just reacted. And, obviously, I reacted poorly. But yes, I'm in love with you. I didn't want to be in love with you. I still don't."

"Why not?" he demanded harshly.

"Because you don't love *me*, Nasir. You have all the power in this relationship. You have from the very beginning. I'm completely vulnerable to you now that you know. You could crush me harder than any of those boys could have. I'm older and, hopefully wiser, but still, you have the power to really hurt me."

He moved closer, his palm reaching out to cup her jaw and cheek. "Never!" he vowed. "You have given me your heart and I will protect that gift just as ferociously as I will protect our child," he told her, his other hand coming to rest on her stomach. "I love you too, Cassandra. From the moment I saw you, I wanted you as my own."

With his words, her heart melted even further! "You love me?" she asked, her voice cracking with the emotions that were swelling up inside of her.

"From the moment I stepped into the conference room that first day," he promised.

"From the first moment?" she teased, feeling light headed, but from happiness this time.

"Don't," he cautioned. "Don't even try to tell me that you didn't feel

118

the same way. From that first moment, we both knew. We could both feel what was happening between us."

He was right and Cassy felt shame for a moment. Then happiness hit her again. "Yes. I felt it as well. I didn't understand it. And, for so long, I've been on the wrong side of male...attention. But the way you looked at me," she lifted her lashes and looked into his eyes, "It was never about my breasts. It was about *me*, wasn't it?"

He nodded, squeezing her fingers. "Always about you, Cassandra. Your breasts are beautiful and I love them. But they don't define you. They have shaped your perception of men in general, but you are a beautiful person inside and out. You are strong and intelligent, funny and fascinating." His eyes dropped to her breasts as a smile crept over his face. "And I love your figure, especially when you aren't wearing one of those horrible sports bras," he teased.

Cassandra couldn't believe his words. She was so happy that she dove into his arms, laughing at his grunt of surprise when he caught her, lifting her up. "I love you," she whispered against his neck.

He lowered his head as well, holding her close. "I love you, Cassandra. Will you please marry me?" he said, this time there was a hint of teasing sarcasm in his voice.

Cassy laughed. "Yes! Yes, I'll marry you."

Epilogue

"You can't do this," Cassy protested as she stepped into Nasir's office.

Nasir leaned back in his leather chair, watching as Cassandra waddled over to his desk. He ignored the document she dropped onto his desk, focusing instead on the beautiful swell of her stomach. "How is our son doing today?" he asked, reaching out to pet her stomach, kissing her belly.

"*She* was annoyed last night," she grumbled, emphasizing the female pronoun.

"I noticed. You tossed and turned all night," he said, standing and kissing her gently. "How is your back?"

Cassy sighed, putting a hand on either side of her bulging tummy. "My back hurts. My boobs hurt. My legs hurt. I'm tired and hungry, but I can't eat anything because of the heartburn that comes after."

Nasir laughed softly as she glared at him. "From past experience, I guess that means that we are about to meet our son?" Their three other boys were wild and rambunctious, and he loved every one of them!

She huffed a bit. "I hope so," she replied, leaning against his hard chest as much as she could. "I'm sick of being pregnant. Next time, *you* get to be pregnant."

He sat back down in his chair, pulling her close. "You've already told me that this is our last child."

Cassy pulled back, shaking her head. "I can't sit on your lap, Nasir. I'm too big. I'll hurt...oomph!" She blinked up at him as he leaned back, steadying her on his thighs. "Well, okay then."

He chuckled at her grumpiness. "You are not too heavy. You are beautiful and we won't have any more children."

She looped her arms around his neck. "You said that the last three times," she groused.

"True," he replied, his hand smoothing down over her very pregnant tummy. "But I'd like to point out that I don't believe that I've been the one to suggest that we have more children."

That was true enough, she thought, glaring at him. "Fine! I'm the one that wanted more! But seriously! Pregnancy sucks!"

"You liked it a few months ago," he teased, nuzzling her neck.

She tilted her head, giving him more room because she liked it when he did that. "Yeah, but that was during the fifth month of this pregnancy. That was when I could still walk and," she gasped when he nipped at her earlobe. "Enjoy sex!" he bit her lobe again, his hands moving higher, cupping her large breasts through the material of her stretchy dress.

"You enjoyed sex last night."

Cassy thought about it and shook her head. "No. I'm too big. It wasn't enjoyable."

"You screamed my name," he reminded her.

She swatted his shoulder and stood up. "A gentleman wouldn't remind me of that," and she walked around to the other side of his desk.

Nasir laughed, his gaze drinking in her pregnant body with appreciation. "Yes, I know. And you know very well that I'm not a gentleman."

Her body warmed and he watched as the blush stole up her cheeks. "I know that too well." She tried to grumble, but her lips curled up into a smile. "Anyway, I should..." Cassy froze, her eyes widening as she looked at Nasir.

"What's wrong?" he demanded, standing up as she gripped her stomach. "Is it the baby?"

Cassy nodded, and looked down at the floor. "My water just broke."

Nasir raced around the desk, pressing a button that alerted the guards stationed outside of his office. He lifted her into his arms as he shouted to the guards, "Get the doctor ready. My wife is in labor!"

There was a great deal of movement and a wheelchair was brought into the office. He put her gently into the chair, then pushed the aide out of the way, determined to get his wife to the delivery room himself.

"Hold on, my love. The doctor has been standing by. You will be..."

"Hurry," Cassy urged, clutching her stomach. "This little girl is ready to join us!" and then she screamed as her first contraction ripped across her abdomen. He pushed her through to the palace delivery ward and Cassy panted through the pain as several nurses helped her onto the delivery room table.

"Tell the kids," Cassy said to Nasir as he stepped out of the way so the nurses could strap on the fetal heart rate monitor over her belly.

121

"I'm not leaving you," he snapped. But he turned to one of the guards. "Tell my sons that their mother is about to give birth to their brother and we will see them later."

The guard nodded, then turned and hurried out of the delivery room.

"Nasir, it hurts!" she yelled, arching her back as another contraction hit her.

The obstetrician came through the doorway, smiling gently as one of the nurses pulled latex gloves over his hands. "Good morning, Your Highness. Apparently, it is time to give this country another heir!" he laughed at his own joke, then moved between Cassandra's legs, feeling for her cervix. "Good grief, you are already fully dilated!"

"I know!" she yelled, fighting to keep from pushing.

The man looked astounded for a moment, then he nodded sharply. "You've delivered three healthy boys. There is nothing to fear."

Cassy gasped for breath as the contraction eased. "Right! Says the *man* who hasn't ever experienced labor."

Nasir pushed her hair out of her eyes. "Honey, you can do this. Our son will join us soon and you will no longer have this..."

She writhed, screaming as another contraction hit. "No! No, no, *no!*"

Nasir wasn't sure what she was objecting to, but figured it was better to be silent.

Five hours later, his fingers were probably broken but he could finally see the head of his son. "Almost there!" the doctor called out over Cassandra's screams. "Just one more big push!"

Cassy shook her head, sweat drenching her hair. "I can't!" she whimpered. But her body took over and she bent at the waist, pushing with all her might.

"There it is!" the doctor called out. "Keep pushing! Keep pushing!"

Cassy screamed, wanting to punch Nasir but the pain and the intense need to push won out. She couldn't seem to do anything other than scream as the pain ripped through her. Moments later, the doctor smiled as her baby gave a soft cry.

"It's a girl!" the doctor announced, grinning from ear to ear.

In the ensuing silence, the nurses, doctor, not to mention Cassy and Nasir, stared at the new arrival.

"A girl!" Cassy whispered, awed and unaware of the tears sliding down her cheeks. "A girl!"

Unfortunately, Cassy was too weak to hold herself up and flopped back against the delivery table. Nasir moved to cut the umbilical cord, then held out his arms to take the tiny girl-child into his arms. A nurse wrapped a cotton blanket around her, and transferred their daughter into dad's arms.

"A girl!' he whispered, moving the cotton blanket out of the way to peer into the wrinkled, furious, red face of his baby girl.

Moving to Cassandra, he lowered his arms so that she could look.

"She's beautiful," Cassy murmured, still trying to recover.

Nasir nodded his agreement. "I love you," and he bent his head to kiss Cassy's forehead.

"I love you, too," she whispered back. "Especially since testosterone didn't win this time!"

He laughed, shaking his head even as he cradled his daughter in his arms. "Our sons are going to..." They both cringed. "I'll hold off on telling them."

Cassy laughed, since their three boys had already been building a fort in which their next brother would live. Yeah, she thought as she watched Nasir cradling their baby girl. Life was pretty darn amazing!

Continue reading for a sneak peek at the final book in The Ladies of The Burling School series

Excerpt to The Secrets of Seduction
Coming July 17, 2020

"Figures," Ella grumbled, staring up at the imposing building that housed the headquarters of Reynolds Industries. Over the past few days, she'd done her research and, although the Duke of Theeds, Edward Reynolds, was still alive, he wasn't active in the social world anymore. But he hadn't passed his title or wealth on to his son, Malcolm Reynolds. In a way, Ella respected Malcolm more because he'd created so much from nothing. He hadn't inherited his wealth, like so many rich aristocrats in the world. He'd created a massive empire through grit and determination. He was thirty-six years old and a billionaire many times over. He bought ailing companies, fixed them up, and sold them off. So he didn't really own anything, other than a huge amount of land and real estate, all of which was separate from his investment company.

And yet, she remembered that shiver of awareness a couple of days ago at the restaurant. The man was tall and arrogant, she thought. But if there was one thing that had never impressed her, it was wealth. In fact, because of the way Edward Reynolds had treated Ella's mother, the way the arrogant jerk had simply tossed her out of his house because he could, his disdain for decades of loyalty and service had caused Ella to despise people with a disproportionate amount of wealth. They had too much power and, in most cases, wielded that power with contemptuous disregard for anyone outside of their social circle.

But staring up at this imposing building, Ella felt...something. Something strange that...well, it wasn't important, she thought. "He's just compensating," she muttered.

"What do you suspect I'm compensating for?" a deep voice asked fom behind her.

Startled, Ella swung around, finding Malcolm Reynolds much closer than she'd anticipated. Much closer and...had he grown a few inches over the past few days? The man was crazy tall! Well over six feet. Ella was five feet, seven inches, so she was relatively tall for a woman. Plus she'd worn black boots with three inch heels. But good grief! Malcolm Reynolds still towered over her!

"What are you doing out here?" she gasped, stepping back to put some space between them.

Those cobalt blue eyes sparkled with amusement, the corners crinkling enticingly. "Am I not supposed to be outside?"

Her eyes narrowed as she realized that he was teasing her. "You're supposed to be inside, destroying people's lives," she retorted with a defiant lift of her chin.

"Ah," he laughed, leaning back slightly. "Well, I broke up ten families this morning, so I thought I'd take a break. Would you like to come inside?" he offered. "We can throw a dart on the wall and see who I should destroy this afternoon. Would be fun...."

Ella bristled at his tone. "This is funny to you?" she demanded, her temper increasing with his mocking attitude.

"A little," he replied with a soft chuckle, putting a hand to the small of her back as he led her into the building. "I think that you are a brilliant reporter, Ella. I've followed your career over the years and I've been impressed with not only by your bravery at reporting on horrible situations, but also your talent at conveying those issues."

He pressed a button on the elevator and, almost immediately, the elevator appeared. With that hand still at her back, he nudged her into the elevator and, they rose. Since this was a glass elevator that looked out at the city, Ella automatically stepped away from the glass and the scary heights. Unfortunately, she stepped back...against him. For a stolen instant, she could feel the hard muscles of his chest against her back and his strong arms around her waist. It was a shocking but pleasant sensation and, since it had been a long time since she'd even kissed a man, it took her a moment to pull away.

"Sorry," she muttered, jerking away from him. But she didn't move too far. The glass of the elevator might be thick, but she didn't trust anything to keep her safe this high above the ground. Unfortunately, that left her standing awkwardly in the middle of the elevator and she almost jumped through the doors when they finally opened on the executive floor.

Breathing deeply, she looked around, trying to calm her racing nerves. Obviously, Ella wasn't a huge fan of heights and she looked up at Malcolm, bracing herself for his amusement at her expense.

"This way," he said and gestured towards one end of the elegantly decorated hallway. No jokes about her fear of heights? No pity or laughter in his eyes? Ella was confused because...he wasn't going to laugh at her?

Reluctantly grateful, Ella followed him down the elegantly decorated hallway, looking around, trying to take in everything as she passed. Feelings, smells, other people's expressions. Everything would be included in her story.

Malcolm paused at an older woman's desk. "Nancy, would you order some lunch for us? We're going to be a while."

Ella frowned. "I'm not staying for lunch," she told him, even though

125

she was famished. She'd skipped breakfast this morning, wanting to check in with her editor before coming to meet with Malcolm.

Nancy ignored Ella and nodded to her boss before turning back to her computer. Order lunch online? That would be excellent! Ella had been out of the country for so long, living in mud huts, tin-roofed houses, or tents...none of which had had reliable internet service. She'd read articles about these conveniences, but since she'd only been back in London for a few days, she hadn't experienced the glory of ordering food from one's phone and having it delivered, hot and yummy, to one's doorstep. Her idea of convenience over the past few years was picking ripe fruit from a tree.

Ella tore her curious eyes away from Nancy's computer and hurried after Malcolm into the office.

"Close the door," Malcolm ordered.

Ella had to restrain herself from slamming it while curtsying. Sarcastically, of course. But she stepped back and quietly closed the door, then turned to face the man she was going to put into prison.

"So..."

"I read that story you did on last month on human trafficking. It was brilliant. Do you think it will do any good?"

Ella had written about the desperate situation in several countries, which created an environment where teenage girls could be enticed to apply for "jobs" in other countries. Unfortunately, the modeling jobs, nanny positions, and housekeeping roles never materialized. Instead, those vulnerable girls were forced into horrible situations, beaten and drugged, sold off as prostitutes, and never seen by their families again. Most of them died and were simply tossed into the streets or a pit somewhere out of the way, easily replaced by yet another girl trying desperately to "make it" in the world.

"I don't know. I ensured that the articles also ran in the smaller newspapers. So if the article saves even one girl from being kidnapped and used, then that's a good thing."

He nodded sharply, those cobalt blue eyes sharp and intelligent. "I agree. What are you working on now?"

She smiled, sitting down in the club chair across from him. "I've come across some interesting leads for a story that, I suspect, started decades ago. Maybe longer."

"I'm intrigued." He opened his mouth to say more, but a knock sounded and Nancy stepped into the office carrying a full tray. "Thank you, Nancy," Malcolm said and she smiled, set the tray down onto the table between them and walked out quietly, pulling the door closed behind her.

"Please, help yourself," he said, referring to the tray of small sandwiches. There were small plates and fruit along with sodas.

"I'm fine," Ella replied, waving the food away.

"Do you mind if I go ahead? I've been in meetings since early this morning and I'm starving."

Ella shrugged. "Fine by me," she told him, then watched, fascinated as he put several of the small sandwiches onto a plate.

"You were telling me about your next revelation?" he prompted.

"I'm working on putting you and your rich cronies into prison," she announced.

That got a smile out of him and Ella wondered about it. Was he so confident about his social status as an aristocrat that he thought of himself as immune to conviction? Or was he innocent of whatever was going on with the secret society?

"That is really going to put a dent in my social life," he chuckled. "What do you think I've done to warrant a prison sentence?' he asked, leaning back and taking another bite of his sandwich.

Ella watched him, oddly fascinated by his hands. They were strong, with long, deft fingers. What was it about those hands was so interesting?

She jerked her eyes away from his hands and looked up at his features. "Um..." focus! "Have you ever heard or seen a symbol like this one?" she asked, pulling out her notebook and flipping to the page where she'd sketched the flaming hand symbol.

Malcolm leaned forward, his eyes looking over the picture before leaning back. "What does it mean?" he asked.

Ella noticed that he hadn't answered her question. Interesting, she thought. "I don't know what it means. Yet," she paused significantly. "But I'm going to find out, Malcolm."

"Where did you first see that symbol?" he asked.

She shook her head. "Doesn't matter. But what do you know about it?"

"Oh, I'm sure that there are secret societies all over the world, Ella."

She smiled predatorily. "Another evasive answer."

He laughed and Ella ignored the jump of her stomach at the deep, rich sound. "You're not giving me a whole lot to go on. Perhaps if you tell me when you saw the symbol, I might be able to help you a bit more."

She shook her head. "I don't give out my sources, Malcolm. You should know that, being in business and all."

"Being in business isn't nearly as mysterious as investigating crimes, I suspect."

Ella tilted her head, fascinated by his answer. "I would have thought

127

that our jobs were pretty similar. I find out a small bit of information, a thread of mystery. And I keep tugging on that thread, discovering those mysteries. In your line of business, you find a clue that a previously strong company has been mismanaged, am I right?" she asked.

"I hunt down companies that are struggling financially," he confirmed.

"And then you keep tugging, looking at data and financial records, checking on the company's sales and stock values."

"You've done your research well," he replied, setting the now-empty plate on the table. "And you think that this symbol," he pointed his chin towards her notebook still open on the low coffee table, "involves something nefarious, dark, and evil?" he asked. "This is the string at which you are pulling, looking under rocks and behind the curtains to find out what's going on."

She stood up, feeling the need to get away from his distractingly handsome smile. "I'm going to find out what this means, Malcolm," she warned, stuffing her notebook back into her messenger bag. "And I'm going to treat you exactly as you treated my mother when she told your family that she was sick."

He'd stood as well, moving closer to her. "I'm very sorry about what my father did to your mother," he said.

Ella jerked, startled by his words. Looking up into those blue eyes, she felt...something strange again.

Pulling back, she blinked and stepped away from the chair. "Right. Well, it's in the past."

"Is it?" he asked gently. "I remember the day that my mother passed away." His jaw clenched and he shook his head slightly. "My father announced that she'd passed and that the funeral was in three days. He ordered me to wear my dark suit." Malcolm's hands slid into his pockets. "I don't think one ever truly gets over the death of a parent, do we?"

Was he closer now? Ella realized that she'd been staring up into his eyes and hadn't noticed him walking towards her.

"It was...years ago." And yet, she could still remember holding her mother's hand in the hospital, seeing the pain in her eyes as the cancer slowly destroyed her.

Malcolm reached out, brushing a light finger down over her cheek. The touch both burned and soothed...it short-circuited her brain.

"You're quite lovely, Ella," he murmured, almost as if he were talking to himself.

Startled, she looked up into his blue eyes, not sure what to say. Never in her wildest imagination would she have expected him to say something like that. Lovely? She wanted to snort with disbelief. Naya was lovely! Cassy! She was a gorgeous woman! Ella knew that she wasn't ugly, but...she wasn't lovely.

But standing here, in front of Malcolm, for some strange reason, she did feel...oddly beautiful. For all her life, she'd pushed to be smart and brave, to confront the injustices in the world. Never had she felt beautiful. This man... his eyes and his electric touch ...caused her to feel pretty.

Why wasn't she leaving? They were standing there, the silence and tension expanding as they stared into each other's eyes. Ella told herself to walk away. But her feet didn't move.

That's when he did something even more astounding.

Ella watched in stunned fascination as he leaned in and kissed her! His lips, so firm and temptingly commanding, brushed over hers, eliciting a startled response from her own. The tingling in her lips was so astonishing that she forgot to pull away. He did it again and again, his lips brushing back and forth against hers and Ella stood there, taking it. No, not just accepting the kiss...her lips actually moved, actually participated in the kiss!

The ache in her belly and the burning sensation against her lips was so new, so strange that she finally pulled away. For another long moment, she just blinked at him, wondering what the hell had just happened!

"Right," she whispered into the silence.

With that, she turned and walked out of his office, feeling stunned and...tingly. And ashamed! She'd just kissed Malcolm Reynolds! What in the world? Why? Why had she simply stood there? Why hadn't she slapped him and given him some pithy set-down that would humiliate him?

Ella stepped into the elevator, too stunned and confused to even fear the glass-enclosed space as it whisked her silently down to the lobby. Down and away from the man she wanted to see in prison.

The man she'd just...kissed!

Malcolm stared at the now-empty doorway, more intrigued than before as he replayed Ella's soft, trembling response to his kiss. Ella was startlingly beautiful, but also tough and sexy with her tight jeans and black boots. Her messenger bag was scruffy and well worn, but was of obvious quality. Her clothes weren't rumpled, as he'd expected she'd requested a meeting with him. She was...lovely. Her blonde hair was straight and long, shining in the overhead lights. While other women of his acquaintance would have done something to bring his attention to their long hair, flipping it over their shoulder or twirling a lock around their fingers...Ella's hair was brushed but forgotten.

She wore minimal makeup, just a touch of mascara and lipstick. Her skin was soft and creamy, making her appear youthful and strong. She was a capable woman wrapped up in soft femininity that, Malcolm suspected, the lovely Ella tried hard to hide and ignore.

An impossible task, he thought with a chuckle as he stood and walked to his desk. Ella couldn't hide her beauty any more than she could ignore a mystery. It was all part of her lovely package and...he was determined to get to know her better. Ella Fleming had always intrigued him. But now, with maturity and bright determination, she got to him in different ways. She was more than simply a curiosity.

She was a challenge!

Damn, she was beautiful! And smart and didn't give an inch! He liked that about her.

What he didn't like was that she might be getting close to something that he and his friends had been working on for the past several years.

Picking up his phone, he dialed a number. "Jenna," he replied as soon as his friend answered. "I just spoke with Ella Fleming and, apparently, she's onto us." He paused, listening. "Right. But we need to be a bit more discreet. Otherwise, the whole operation could be revealed, which would put our people in danger."

Hanging up, he wondered if...was his father still countering the group's efforts? Were his father and his cronies still active? Malcolm had thought that their efforts had been shut down, but perhaps it was time to make sure.

Made in United States
North Haven, CT
25 October 2023

43213865R00081